Praise for Lucienne Diver

VAMPED

"I really sank my teeth into Lucienne Diver's *Vamped*. A fun, frothy teenage romp with lots of action, a little shopping, and a cute vampire guy. Who could ask for more?"
—Marley Gibson,
author of the Ghost Huntress series

"This book rollicked along, full of humor, romance, and action. Gina is a smart-aleck heroine worth reading about, a sort of teenage Betsy Taylor *(Undead and Unwed)* with a lot of Cher Horowitz *(Clueless)* thrown in. Fans of Katie Maxwell will devour *Vamped*."
—Rosemary Clement-Moore,
author of *Texas Gothic*

"Move over, Buffy! Lucienne Diver transfuses some fresh blood into the vampire genre. Feisty, fashionable, and fun—*Vamped* is a story readers will sink their teeth into and finish thirsty for more."
—Mari Mancusi,
author of the Blood Coven Vampires series

"Those who enjoy a good giggle will respond eagerly to this brassy, campy romp."
—*Kirkus Reviews*

"Teenagers will likely bite at the fun premise of Diver's YA debut."

—*Publishers Weekly*

"A lighthearted, action-packed vampire romance story following in the vein of Julie Kenner's *Good Ghouls*, Marlene Perez's *Dead*, and Rachel Caine's The Morganville Vampires series."

—*School Library Journal*

"Diver uses wit and adventure to hook readers with this teen vampire story, and the novel gives teen girls plenty of romance."

—*VOYA*

ReVamped

"Thoroughly enjoyable, this sequel is a light, fizzy read. Listening in on Gina's thoughts and quick-witted dialogue is what makes this such a treat."

—*Kirkus Review*s

"*ReVamped* by Lucienne Diver was witty, sweet, and just dark enough to ignite my morbid taste buds."

—Bitten by Books

"Perfect for teens and adults, this is a book to share, savor and revisit. *ReVamped* is full of smart, spot-on dialogue, engaging, authentic characters and a plot that's so much fun it's impossible not get swept up."

—*Examiner.com*

Lucienne Diver

fangtastic

flux
TM
Woodbury, Minnesota

First Edition
First Printing, 2012

Book design by Bob Gaul
Cover design by Lisa Novak
Cover art: Woman © Mixa/PunchStock,
Night club scene © iStockphoto.com/dwphotos

Flux, an imprint of Llewellyn Worldwide Ltd.

Library of Congress Cataloging-in-Publication Data
Diver, Lucienne, 1971–
    Fangtastic / Lucienne Diver.—1st ed.
        p. cm.—(Vamped ; #3)
    Summary: Gina and her boyfriend, both vampires working undercover for the government, are sent to investigate a group of humans who act like vampires and have been on a killing spree in Tampa, Florida.
    ISBN 978-0-7387-3039-4
    [1. Vampires—Fiction. 2. Spies—Fiction. 3. Florida—Fiction.] I. Title.
    PZ7.D6314Fan 2012
    [Fic]—dc23

                                                        2011028802

                                    Flux
                        Llewellyn Worldwide Ltd.
                            2143 Wooddale Drive
                        Woodbury, MN 55125-2989
                            www.fluxnow.com

                Printed in the United States of America

Acknowledgments

There are so many people to whom I want to express appreciation, and so little room to do it. First, thank you to my awesome husband, Pete, and son, Ty, for all the encouragement and love; my entire family for support and inspiration; Joy Heuser for helping me scout locations; Beth Dunne for keeping me laughing; and Don (Vlad) Deich for amazingly valuable information. (Note: while there is a Vlad in *Fangtastic*, the real deal is much more Snape-eque, if I can create my own entirely fictitious word. Survey says?) Also, I'm sending a huge thank you to my agent, Kristin Nelson, and her incredible team, as well as the entire Flux crew for helping me bring Gina and her peeps to "life."

Finally, I want to give a mega shout out to my fans, especially those who write. I love hearing from you!

For Ty, Kaleb, Mikey, Cameron and all the boys this time

Vampire Dictionary for the
Grave-ly Uninformed by Gina Covello

OMG, nobody told me vampdom came with a vocabulary list! Apparently, if you're a human who wants to walk the walk, you've got to talk the talk ... or something like that. So, if you're still alive and kicking but want to play on the shady side of the street, you're going to need your very own vampirism cheat sheet. Ever helpful, I've provided some vocab words below. And yes, you will be tested on this later.

- *The Black Veil* (which I look totally hot in, by the way): Turns out this isn't so much a fashion statement as some kind of code. Words to live by. Kinda like a vamp version of *Cosmo* ... only different.

- *Roleplayer/lifestyler:* Not the guy who still lives with his parents and pays way more attention to *World of Warcraft* than his own personal hygiene. Someone who likes to dress up and play vampire.

- *Sanguines:* People who put on their prosthetic teeth or otherwise open a vein to feed. (Really? I mean, with mochachinos and milkshakes in the world, you're opting for blood? If I had the choice, I'd be going after a little thing I like to call taste.)

- *Pranic or psychic vampires:* Feng shui vamps. They feed on life force instead of blood.

- *Fledgelings:* Humans new to the "vampire" court. Someday they might leave the nest and establish their own clutch, clan, or coven. Or not.

- *Elder:* If you've served the community well you may be selected to become an elder. I'm sorry, but one of the primo things about being a vampire, even if you only play one on TV, is eternal youth. "Elder" is too much like "older"—just takes all the fun out of things.

- *Knighted Ronan:* Kinda like black knights. Respect, yo, but no definite loyalties, no politics.

- *Regent:* Prom king and/or queen of the vampire court.

- *Clan or House:* Like a fanged fraternity or a sanguine sorority. (Note how I was actually able to use the word "sanguine" in a sentence. Points for me!)

Other terms you might need:

- *Telemetric:* A person who can read the history of an object by touch.

- *Telekinetic:* Someone who can move objects with their mind. Great fun at parties ... and séances.

- *Telepath:* Someone with the ability to read minds as easily as the latest issue of *Vogue.* Also to send mental messages.

- *Truth-teller:* Like a living lie detector, a guy or gal who magically knows whether you've been naughty or nice.

1

Okay, I'd only been on one super-secret spy mission for the Feds so far and already I knew my favorite part—the downtime afterward.

My BFF Marcy and I were sitting on the world's least comfortable couch in the rec room at spook central giving each other pedicures and catching up on missed episodes of *Project Runway*. We were both in drawstring shorts and tanks, though I filled my top out better. To compensate, she had her shorts rolled down low enough to show her tramp stamp. Not that there was anyone around to see us. Just about everyone else was super serious and busy, busy, busy. They couldn't appreciate that sometimes you had to sit back and smell the nail polish. Ultraviolet in my case; Tantalizing Tangerine for Marcy.

Cosmetic companies were big on that alliteration. Big word, huh—"alliteration." I learned it from my boy Bobby. Did I mention that he's a genius? Or the near clone of Zac Efron? For Twilighters—Edward who?

"Okay, gimme your other foot," I told her as I finished the first.

Marcy shifted on the couch so she could swing her painted foot onto the coffee table and bring her untouched toes my way, and suddenly the channel changed from Renee's big reveal to news.

We both groaned, and Marcy reached beneath herself for the remote she was sitting on when I halted her.

"Wait, turn it up."

Out of the corner of my eye, I caught the funny look she gave me. The rest of my attention was riveted on the television, where I thought they'd just said something about vampires. The footage they were showing was really blurry, as if the show's producers had done their best to enlarge a distant shot. But there was definitely something man-shaped in the picture, silhouetted against an outside wall—with what looked like a giant tarantula on his head, but was probably a mousse job gone horribly wrong. He made some sort of sign at the camera and ran off into the night. A second shadow followed in his wake.

"Witnesses say—" a newscaster blared suddenly.

I winced at the volume. "I didn't say turn it up full blast!"

"Sorry!"

Marcy got the volume back under control. I missed what it was the witnesses said, but then heard, "Police called to the home found a scene of carnage and have just now released the names of the victims—forty-nine-year-old Jonathan Swinter and forty-two-year-old mother-of-two Margo Beckett Swinter. Their youngest daughter is reported to be in critical condition. Their eldest daughter, who sources say was not living at home at the time of the attack, has not yet been located. Police have set up a tip line and are asking that anyone with information—"

"What's up?" Marcy asked. "You know them?"

"No, but—"

"Meeting." Leaning in the doorway was a square-faced young stud with dark, military-short hair and no lips—not to speak of, anyway. In keeping with my "S" nicknaming scheme for our government handlers, I'd dubbed him Agent Straight-laced. But apparently his real name was Brent.

"But our toes," Marcy protested. "Can't it wait until they're dry?"

"Let me think. Death, destruction, national security... um, no."

"Yeah, well, my very cover could depend on the even application of polish. The slightest imperfection could give me away. I don't want to call that kind of attention to myself," Marcy said.

"Then maybe you should roll up your shorts," he suggested.

"Okay, you two," I cut in, "get a room." I swung my feet down to the floor and rose, but pedicure sandals were so not meant for graceful exits.

"What—never!" Marcy sputtered.

"Maybe if it were the end of the world," Brent said, about the same time.

"In your dreams!" Marcy fired back.

His eyes flared. "Oh, you've no idea."

Yup, I'd called it. No one could be that straight-laced *and* sane. One or the other had to give. Since the Feds probably did psych evals on their employees, I was guessing Marcy made him nuts in the *me Tarzan, you Jane* way rather than the *American Psycho* way. They were fun to poke at.

"After you," Brent said, indicating the door. He might have wanted to make sure we didn't dawdle, but I thought it was to get a better look at Marcy's tramp stamp. It was a good thing Marcy had used a fake ID to get the tat on her sixteenth birthday, because now that we'd been vamped, body alterations wouldn't take—not tattoos, piercings, or Botox. Anything alien or perforating got pushed out and healed up. If it weren't for the whole eternal-youth thing, the rest would probably have sent me screaming into the night. Luckily, though, my lips had never needed collagen injections, and our all-liquid diet was very slimming.

Marcy followed me out of the room, both of our feet flapping like ducks'. Pedicure sandals were a little like flip-flops, but with partitions between *each* toe, not just the first and second. Difficult to manage sashaying down hallways, but as I looked back, Marcy was doing her best. I wondered if she was quite as indifferent to Agent Straight-laced as she pretended. With Marcy it was hard to tell; the swing in her step was as unconscious as breathing … even more so now that breath was no longer a factor.

"Briefing room four," Brent called from behind us.

I pushed through the door on the right into a room that would send high school AV squads to geek heaven. There were screens, projectors, gadgets, doodads ... I didn't even know what half the stuff did, but I immediately recognized the image on the central screen. Marcy and I had just seen it on TV—the blurry figure from the newscast. How random was that?

Bobby was already there, seated front and center like the teacher's pet that he was. He'd been one of the brains back at our old school, and while that hadn't changed, the loss of his Coke-bottle lenses had let me see him in a whole new light. Especially his unbelievable blue eyes. The wicked vamp powers didn't hurt either. He had mojo out the wazoo ... okay, that sounded so, so wrong. Mojo to spare ... there, that sounded better. Anyway, he was smokin' hot, plenty powerful, and *mine*.

He took my hand as I sat and gave it a squeeze. It sent a kind of electric shock through me, straight to my heart, which did a little stutter like it might restart.

On either side of the screen stood Agent Stuffed Shirt— aka Sid, and Agent Stick-up-her-butt—aka Maya, who rolled her eyes at the sight of our hand-holding. Probably she thought it was unprofessional. Whatever. Neither of us had volunteered to work for the Feds. They'd made us an offer we couldn't refuse. Literally. So making her crazy was sort of one of the perks of the job.

I was surprised when, instead of going off on his merry way, Brent closed the door behind him and joined us at the table. Marcy, Bobby, and I were all part of the juju brigade—a group of vamps who'd been recruited to handle supernatural spy stuff—but Brent was a breather, just like all the handlers I'd seen so far. I wondered if that was significant, like there was some kind of bias against vamps being in positions of power.

Before I could pursue this thought, Maya tossed folders down in front of each of us. "Already?" I grumbled. "We've only had a week to recover from our last mission."

"You're super-speedy healers. How much time do you need? Besides, after you've given yourselves manicures, pedicures, facials, bikini waxes, and all the rest of that crap, what else is left?"

"You know, a massage would be really soothing."

She growled.

"Jeez, lighten up. I was thinking for *you*. Hot stone massage, maybe. And a paraffin dip for your hands, because damn, woman—"

"Enough!" Sid said from the front of the room. "We have a case. While you vamps may live forever, these people ... " He threw a set of eight-by-ten color glossies down on the table. As if he'd practiced, they fanned out perfectly. "These people didn't. And we don't think the folks who did this are anywhere near done."

Bobby picked up the nearest photo, which looked like a still from some horror flick. I glanced away, but not before I saw a woman with her throat slashed, her shirt torn open, and enough spilled blood to paint the walls, which someone had done, forming the word *VICTIM* all in caps. Okay, so the baddies had mastered the obvious and for some reason felt the need to share with the class.

"This is awful, but it looks like a normal killing, if there is such a thing. Isn't this a job for local police or maybe the FBI? Why get us involved?" Bobby asked.

"A witness reported that the perpetrators were vampires." Sid held up a hand to stop Bobby's oncoming protest. "Of

course, we know they're not. For one thing, they were ‹
on camera skulking around the house. For another—"

"Vampires would never have wasted all that blood," Bobby
cut in, unable to resist.

"Right." Sid picked up a clicker from a nearby TV stand
and the image onscreen changed to a closer-in shot of that
central figure. It was sharper, too, like it had been enhanced.
"However, we've identified one of the suspects as Nelson Ricci,
a seventeen-year-old high school senior. He actually is part of
the Tampa vampire community—the human vampire community—where he goes by the name of Dion. We assume that the
others with him come from the same group." Sid clicked over
to a screen shot of the second shadow Marcy and I had noticed
in the news footage. No amount of enhancement could turn a
shadow into a mug shot, but it was clear that the shade had a
few too many limbs, meaning it probably showed at least two
people running side by side.

"Dion?" I mused. As vamp names went, it was hardly as
awe-inspiring as Grigori or even Edward. It sounded more diva
than devil.

"There's a vampire community in Tampa?" Bobby asked
at the same time. "As in Tampa, *Florida*? The Sunshine State?
And this community lets in humans? I think my head might
just explode."

"If you would all stop interrupting," Sid said stiffly, living up to his Stuffed Shirt label, "I'll get to all that." He took
a breath, as if he were planning to get the info out in one
shot before anyone had another chance to cut in. "Yes, there's
a vampire clutch in Tampa, *Florida*, made up of people who
behave like vampires—both energy vampires and bloodsuckers

with prosthetic fangs. The thing is that the people who run the clubs and parties for these humans are the real thing. Hiding in plain sight, making money and feeding from willing donors who have no idea of the truth and would only be intrigued by it if they did."

"Brilliant!" Bobby said.

"I'm so glad you approve," Sid answered wryly. *"Anyway,* our plan is twofold. We want to find these killer kids and, if we can, infiltrate the true vampire community. We're going in hard and soft. Gina, all of vampiredom knows about you because of the council's Kill or Capture order. We're going to use that to our advantage. You're going to go in, ask questions, snoop. Don't be too obvious, but don't be a wallflower either."

I snorted. Like that was even a possibility.

"We want the vampires to notice you," he continued, "and to bring you into the fold."

"But—" Bobby started to protest.

Sid just talked over him. "Don't worry. They won't kill her. She's going to offer them something they want very badly." We all looked at him expectantly. *"You."*

My jaw dropped and an objection formed on my lips, but Sid was already moving on. "Gina, you're going to pose as a double agent. Tell them you're finished working for the Feds. Too many rules and regulations, the pay is lousy…improvise. Convince them you can turn Bobby to their side as well, bring him in as a show of good faith. Once you're both on the inside, gather all the intelligence you can. We have reason to believe that the vampire council has hatched a new plan. We need to know what they're up to and locate their base of operations so we can stop them."

"And you think the council is sharing their secrets with the club-running vamps of Tampa Bay?" I asked.

"I think that once you get Bobby to them, you and he will be passed quickly up the chain of command to those in the know."

"Um … yay?"

"Marcy and Brent," Sid continued without pause, "will be soft surveillance. While Gina's getting in good with the vamps, we want you two out there mingling with the patrons. Find out who associates or is associated with the killer kids. Talk to them. You're on the human element, but you're also to back up Bobby and Gina as your investigation allows. Their primary concern will be the vampire power players. However, it seems likely the two are connected. We need to find out how."

"And catch the killers, of course," Bobby cut in.

"Of course," Sid said smoothly, in a way that made it sound like *whatever*. "Solve the murders, bring down the vamps. Simple and straightforward."

Yeah, and if we believed that, he probably had a bridge we could buy, somewhere in Brooklyn …

"What am I supposed to be doing while Gina baits me on a hook and dangles me in front of the vamps?" Bobby asked. "Why can't we both go to them?"

"If you both go, they've got you. No reason to trust when they can lock you away as prisoners. But if Gina convinces them that you and she are on their side by bringing you in, you'll have the freedom you need to get to the truth. In the meantime, you're with us. We'll keep you close so that the vamps can't get to you directly. You'll help us with background checks, looking into Nelson Ricci's known associates.

Both his parents are dead. He lives with an eccentric uncle, who the police so far have been unable to contact. We need to track him down, along with the missing Swinter girl—there's a chance she's involved. We've arranged things with local law enforcement. Our official story is that we're part of a task force to identify and stop burgeoning serial killers."

Marcy raised her hand like we were back in school.

"Yes, Marcy?" Maya said with a half-roll of her eyes.

"One question. How's Mr. Military here going to fit into the vampire scene?" Marcy tipped her head toward Brent. "He totally screams *government*."

Maya gave a grin worthy of a shark, an animal with hundreds, maybe thousands, more pointy teeth than a vamp. "Oh, you won't even recognize him when we're through. The next vampire ball is two nights away. You've got that long to learn all you can about the vampire subculture."

Which sounded so weird, because, of course, we were the vampire subculture, such as it was.

2

M arcy and Brent (now going by their vampire names of Raven and Mal) were already inside the club. The Feds had faked a message from a human vamp—which Bobby said was an oxymoron, but I never knew there were different types—from a New York clan to a lifesty-ler on the Tampa scene. The message vouched for Raven and Mal, gaining them a native guide and instant entrée. And Maya had been right. If Brent hadn't been standing next to Marcy, who looked like a goth French maid—in a white off-the-shoulder blouse, shiny black waist-cincher, and a crinolined skirt that belled out like a tutu—I'd never have recognized him. The Feds' twisted stylists had shaved Brent's head and tattooed it with a web design over his entire cranium, bringing it to a point like a widow's peak on his forehead. A spider hung from an inked thread down the back of his neck. It freaked me out, but I couldn't imagine the tat was permanent.

Me? I'd sink or swim on my own. If—when—I was discovered, no one was going down with me. Marcy and Brent were supposed to focus more on the breathers than the biters, me included. So, for one of the first times in my life, I actually had to wait in *line* behind the velvet ropes, hoping for the nod that would get me into the club. On the upside, I was smokin' hot … and I say that in all honesty. A vivid purple corset pushed and smooshed my cleavage into a shelf just below my shoulders with a tiny lavender rosebud tucked in the center, maybe for modesty. My skirt hit the top of my spiked heels, but when I walked, the side slits exposed me all the way to the hip, which, given the contrast between the dark skirt and my lily-white skin, was pretty obvious. And—brace yourselves—I'd made sure there were no VPL (visible panty lines, for those playing at home). My hair was crimped and teased to epic proportions, with two kicky pigtails on either side draped in black tulle and violet ribbons. To fit in and give myself a little anonymity, I had pale pancake makeup on my face, dark smoky eyes, blood-red lips, and a fake nose ring.

Turns out I was overdressed. A police cruiser was parked on the street, watching for trouble, maybe because of Dion the Destroyer. I was surprised the policemen weren't arresting people for indecent exposure. There were a few outfits that looked like they were held together by nothing more than duct tape and dental floss. Whoever'd said that "less is more" had no idea how sexy it is to leave something up to the imagination. At least any butt cracks were obscured by faux raccoon tails, and the lack of clothing generally made it easier to detect pulse points.

Maybe I could find my "in" as a stylist for the damned. Or the darned, anyway, 'cause these kids were definitely still alive and kicking.

The club itself was pretty industrial looking from the outside, like it had once been a warehouse. The only indications that it was now a goth club, besides the loitering, were the blacked-out windows and the blood-red awning with square cut-outs at the bottom, like castle ramparts. There was a black silhouette of a tower painted dead center, with a raven circling its heights.

Tired of waiting, I was about to skirt the line and offer the bouncer at the door a sniff of my rosebud when there came a stir from the street. The others in line with me turned, craning their necks for a view.

I gasped and fell back a step before shaking it off and regaining my rightful place against the velvet rope, cleavage up front and center.

There they were. The beautiful people. I didn't care if they were biters or bleeders. At that moment, I wanted to be them.

Leading the way was a man in a top hat, tails, and cravat, the chain of a pocket watch stretched from one side of his jacket to the other. And the buttons on the jacket ... clockwork-looking gears. In one gloved hand he carried a cane, the bulb of which glinted gold in the outside lighting. He should have looked silly, affected, out of place, but something about the way he carried it off almost seemed to transform the world around him to mesh with his reality. He'd make a helluva vampire if he wasn't one already. Given his layers of clothing, I couldn't tell if he still breathed, and, contrary to so much fiction, we didn't get any kind of mystical zing at the sight of each other.

A step behind him walked a woman in a clockwork bustier. There was no other way to describe it. A clock face covered her chest, moving gears exposed to sight with nary a connecting cloth to be seen. It couldn't have been comfortable. Her skirt, to make up for it, had enough flounces and fabric for three, including a bustle, kind of like a Bump-it for the butt. There were others behind her: a woman in an iridescent dress adorned with peacock plumes, who was wearing a veiled hat and carrying a lacy parasol over her shoulder, was followed by another woman dressed something like a tarted-up Amelia Earhart, a man who looked like an old-time explorer, and another man dressed as a maharajah.

"The Burgess Brigade," a voice said from behind me, far too close to my ear. "Steampunk vampires."

Darn vamp senses didn't do me a bit of good if I was totally distracted. I turned and almost bumped noses with a startlingly attractive guy. He hadn't been there moments before; I'd swear it. Even with my enhanced vision, I could just barely tell that his eyes weren't completely black, but the glowering gray of storm clouds. His hair was long, wavy, and free-flowing, blacker even than his eyes. His chin was pointed, his face was narrow, almost foxlike, and he had the kind of cheekbones models starved for. In fact, he looked more the tortured poet than the guys I usually went for—guys more focused on me than melancholy. But he did have the older-guy caché going for him. I figured him for twenty-one—twenty-two at the outside.

"Yeah?" I asked, refusing to give ground. It might have been a mistake. I'd fed before coming, but my new friend's open-necked shirt, which tucked down into lace-up leather pants, left no doubt that he was a breather. I could see the pulse point on his neck, and it called to me like the window display at Macy's.

"Yeah. One of our premier clans. You want an introduction?"

I didn't want to seem *too* anxious for the help. "Are you one of them?"

"I, my lady," he said, taking my hand and bringing it to his lips, "am Ballard." He breathed across my knuckles, but aside from where his hand held mine, he didn't so much as touch me. I tried to keep a straight face at the old-fashionedness of it. If Ballard held doors, paid for dates, and bought extravagant gifts, Bobby might have a run for his money.

"And I'm what's known in Greek parlance as a GDI," he added.

"GDI?"

"God-damned independent. In vampire terms, a knighted ronan."

"Oh, right," I answered, thinking quickly back to my vampire vocab. "Knighted ronan" equaled free agent. No clan connection. "And Ballard?"

"As in J. G. Ballard. The writer."

"Oh," I said again, hoping he wasn't after me for my mind, because it didn't seem like it planned to make a showing tonight. I had totally no idea who this J. G. guy was—or even if it was a guy. You never could tell with initials.

"Shall we?" he asked, tucking my hand through his arm without waiting for my response. Shades of Ulric, the goth guy from my last mission, rose up, and my lips twitched. I still thought about him every once in a while, wondering what he was up to. No good was almost a certainty.

"I've done something right?" Ballard asked, at the sight of my smile.

"You've rescued me from this line, haven't you?"

He smiled back at me, and I caught a glimpse of his fake fangs. I wondered how cool I'd be if I showed off the real thing.

I'm in, I sent mentally to Bobby. The whole telepathy thing was his mojo, not mine, so he had to be tuned in to my wavelength to hear me. Apparently he had more important things to focus on, because I didn't get an answer.

Together with a few "excuse me's," some more pointed than others, we made our way to the front of the line. Some people gave us dirty looks, but others didn't dare, waiting to see if we were members of the in-crowd before alienating us. When we got to the bleached-blond vampiress checking IDs and taking cover charges at the front, she took one look at Ballard through her cat's-eye contact lenses and launched into a full body hug, all of her parts completely flush with his. If he and I were an actual item, I'd have had to take her down.

"She with you?" cat-woman asked, belatedly giving me a once-over.

"She is."

She sighed. "ID?"

I slid it out of my cleavage, which widened Ballard's smile to wolfish. Cat-woman didn't react as she slid the ID beneath a reader and passed it back to me. She stamped our hands with a bat symbol. *Very vamp.* Ballard hustled me off before I could pay my cover charge. Apparently, he had privileges.

"I never got your name," he said, steering me away from the front door and up a spiral staircase directly before us. There were rooms off to the left and right that I'd have to explore later, but for now . . .

Well, the name on my ID would be Gail Kuttner, but in the vampire culture I'd go as—"Cosette."

"Ah, from *Les Misérables.*"

I nodded. I'd been prepped about the origin of my name, but all I really remembered was that she was tragic and French. I hoped that would be enough.

"Well, Cosette, for the privilege of escaping the queue and the cover charge and for my aid in your introductions, you get to buy our first round," Ballard said, eyes sparkling as he guided me toward the second floor bar. I just knew there'd be a catch. Clearly, it wasn't my mind but my money that appealed to him. Although, given the glances he snuck at my cleavage, maybe that wasn't it entirely.

To his credit, at least he didn't order a really expensive drink, just an amber ale. Amateur.

"Nothing for you?" Ballard asked as I paid the bartender and handed him his beer.

"I prefer live donors," I said in complete seriousness.

"Whoa, slow down. We've only just met."

"I never said I'd chosen you," I answered, showing a smile

with just a hint of true fang to make it seem like a challenge rather than a diss.

He bowed to me, careful to keep his beer upright, and straightened with a smile. "Well then, m'lady, I suppose I must prove my worth."

I so wanted to launch right into asking him about the killer kids or the club's illuminati, but it would seem too abrupt and I wasn't ready to draw suspicion just yet. There was still a lot of recon to consider. The sheer size of the Tower was daunting. I'd seen another staircase leading up, so there were at least three floors of nearly wall-to-wall people. The floor we were now on had mock stone walls and heavy wooden beams, giving the place a dungeonlike look. Here and there were red pennants or banners for a splash of color, which was good, because the predominant palette for the clientele was black—leather, pleather, vinyl, latex, silk, lace... Occasionally, there was midnight blue, maybe even red or hot pink.

I pointed to a group dancing in bulk out on the dance floor. They wore club clothes, more or less (but mostly less), and sparkled under the sparse lights like fictional vamps in sunshine.

"Who are they?" I asked.

"Glitter goths," he answered with a smirk.

"And them?" I nodded toward a threesome that went by, headed toward the bar. The girls were in spiky boots, black bikini tops, and short skirts, the boy bare-chested in jeans with a silver-studded belt and matching studs on his biker boots.

"Tourists."

"Ah." I wished I did have a drink to sip. People-watching was thirsty work, especially with so many veins exposed.

I was just about to ask another question when a girl slunk up to us in what looked like an emerald negligee and glass slippers. She slid a hand over Ballard's chest and circled around behind him, the hand sliding from his chest down to his stomach as she rested her chin on his shoulder to stare at me.

"Another newbie?" she asked.

Thanks to my vamp-o-vision, I could see even in the club's low lighting that her eyes were the same shade as her gown ... nearly the same color as my own, although my eyes were a touch brighter. Hers were the deep green of, yes, emeralds, or shiny new leaves. Mine were the paler, totally more luminescent green of jade or aventurine. She blinked at me— surprised, I thought. Truly green eyes were rare.

"As you were once," Ballard answered her. He sighed when she didn't move along. "Mina, meet Cosette. Cosette, Mina."

She held out the hand that had been stroking Ballard's stomach for me to shake.

I accepted it, appreciating how well the green polish with black accents matched her dress, much like my ultraviolet went with my corset. A girl after my own unbeating heart. Mina shook, but when I tried to pull back, she refused to let me go. Instead, she slid out from behind Ballard to tuck my hand through her arm, as he himself had done earlier.

"What are your plans with this one?" she asked.

"She wants an introduction to the Burgess Brigade."

"Ah." Mina looked me over, disconcertingly close. "Are you an aviatrix? An inventor? A doxy?"

My mouth might have fallen open. "Uh, I don't think so."

"Then they won't have you. Come, I know who will. He's a collector, of sorts, and you are just his type."

"Mina," Ballard growled, like a warning. "Back off."

"But darling, surely you meant to present her to the Regent." There was a warning to her voice as well. If I hadn't been used to dealing with actual vamps, who could put some mesmeric mojo behind their words, the whole thing might have seemed a lot more ominous.

Ballard didn't look too happy about it, but he followed along beside Mina as she dragged me off through the throngs of people.

The hard-hitting beat of the music seemed to die down as we ascended the staircase to the third floor. We could almost talk without shouting or getting up-close-and-personal with each other's earwax.

"What's upstairs?" I asked.

Mina swiveled her head to share an amused look with Ballard. "She really is a newbie, isn't she?"

"Asked and answered," he said, more like a lawyer than the writer he was named for.

"The court, darling," she answered then, stroking my arm so lingeringly that I wondered if she was entirely straight. "I want you to meet Vlad … or, more specifically, I want *him* to meet *you*."

I looked back at Ballard as if he were my touchstone, since I'd known him a whole quarter-hour longer. I knew about the human vampire court, of course. It had been part of the Feds' crash course in Vamp Culture 101, but *Vlad*? As in Vlad Drakul? Since the clubbers weren't supposed to know about the true vamps, surely not. Vlad had to be just another pseudonym, like Mina, Ballard, or Cosette, and not the real thing … although that would be wicked cool.

"So, the court—that's where you bring up issues, settle disputes and all that, right?" I asked. "Figure out how to deal with public relations disasters?"

Mina's steps slowed and stopped, to the frustration of the people behind us on the staircase, who clucked disapprovingly and went around, shooting us meaningful glares.

"Public relations disasters?" she said through clenched teeth. "Like—"

I pulled my hand from her arm, not about to play this all meek and backpedaly. "Oh, come on, the story's been all over the news. The cult, or whatever, of kids that killed that family. Witnesses are saying they're vampires."

Ballard snorted. Mina's eyes narrowed as she watched me like a hawk who'd spotted movement and hadn't yet decided if it was worth the effort to swoop in. "You're not press, are you?"

I looked down at myself—cleavage, rosebud, skirt slit to my nonexistent skivvies. "Do I *look* like a reporter?"

"She's got you there," Ballard said with a laugh.

Mina's face relaxed. "PR nightmare, yes, but those kids aren't with us. In fact, the one whose face is all over the news—Dion—he was banished. Definitely not one of us."

"Okay," I answered. "Sorry if I offended. I just figured that's why the cops were parked out front and all, because of some connection. I didn't know the topic was taboo."

"More like closed," Ballard said, stepping up between Mina and me and offering his arm to get us on the move again. "We've told the police everything we know."

"So why are they staking the place out?" I asked, pushing it, but, you know—no guts, no glory.

"Since we banished Dion, they think he might target us in revenge. They're here for our protection ... or so they say."

"You don't believe it?"

Ballard's storm-gray eyes were whipped up to hurricane-level ominous. "I think we were as bad a fit for Dion as he was for us. He had some very peculiar ideas. Seems he found others who didn't find those ideas quite so bizarre."

I totally wanted to hear more about those "peculiar ideas," but we were at the top of the stairs now and moving through a curtain of gauzy black streamers into the turret part of the Tower. There sat a man on what looked like an actual throne, all gnarled wood with the burls and knots seeming to form faces that peered out at us. I was so taken with the chair that I hardly noticed the man at first. Ulric and the gang from Maureen Benson High would practically have killed for that chair. I almost wouldn't blame them. Truly, it was fit for a scream queen ... or king.

I only tore my gaze away when I became aware of all the other eyes on me. I looked around the gathering. The Burgess Brigade was there, bright and beautiful, but there were other groups, like the all-female gang that looked like semi-classic gangstas—fedoras, blood-red lips, pinstriped shirts opened all the way down to the top button of their tight vests. Some wore painted-on pants, others short skirts. All were in stiletto-heeled boots. My loyalties immediately swung their way. If I ended up among the vampire lifestylers for any period of time, I wanted to be a gangst-her.

The assembly didn't stay focused on me for long before all eyes turned back to the figure on that gnarly chair, the throne. My gaze was drawn right along with them, up into the electric-blue gaze of the stunning man seated there. He was staring back at me, and the contact gave me a little "hello, hottie" zing of awareness. Clearly, I was a sucker for blue eyes ... his, Bobby's ... though these were set off with some serious guyliner that really made them pop. Also, where Bobby's hair was shaggy brown, all boy-band badass, the royal vamp's was sleek and blond, pulled back into a ponytail at the base of his neck. He was dressed in all black, from the open-necked shirt to the leather duster he had to be roasting in to the ebony pants tucked into fold-over boots. Now, to the fashion-challenged, black is black is black, but anyone who truly *cares* knows just how wrong that is. Getting your blacks to match, even to the point where vamp-o-vision could barely tell them apart, is a feat worthy of a master. It was a talent I could respect. The Tampa human-vampire community seriously needed to put him on recruiting posters. Based on the capacity crowd, maybe they already had.

"Bingo," Mina said, a laugh in her voice. "Vlad, Ballard and I are pleased to present to you Cosette." She glanced over at Ballard, who now looked totally resigned. "Cosette, may I introduce you to our Regent, Vlad Drakul." *Bingo!* Half an hour in and already I'd gone straight to the top ... of the human community, anyway.

I was sort of on my own from here on out. The Feds had only known so much about how the court ran. Apparently, the first rule of Bite Club was that you don't talk about Bite Club. There wasn't a whole lot of info just floating out there for the taking. But it seemed natural, when faced with a figure on a throne, to drop into a curtsey. If nothing else, it gave all the gathered guys a sneak peek straight down the front of my corset, except for the part covered by my demur little rose. If the curtsey wasn't right, at least it would be memorable.

When I looked up, Vlad was staring at the rosebud like he could laser it gone. Yup, I still had it.

"Come," he said, holding out a hand for me to take, "stand beside us as we complete our business." The royal "we," I wondered?

I rose from the curtsey and glided forward to take his hand, which he used to guide me over to his left, to where the Burgess Brigade held court. The peacock lady and the explorer—who looked like Indiana Jones, his sandy-brown hair a shade lighter than his outfit—made room for me. He gave me the once-over with interest, but she snapped open her fan to half hide her face, eyes glittering like diamond-studded daggers above the black lace. The others present studied me as well, with varying reactions ranging from speculation to hostility. I got the sense that Vlad had just shown me some sort of approval and that the others were trying to figure out how it might affect their standing. I supposed I should be all aflutter. Since I'd been vamped, the only way I could see myself was through the appreciation in others' eyes; I was as vain as the next vamp who'd tried to turn her own stylist and start an entourage.

Things got really boring after that. This person or that would propose another person I didn't know for knighting or eldering or whatever. The latter seemed particularly unappealing. All I could picture was someone withering on contact—coquette to crone in zero to sixty.

I couldn't have been the only one bored. People shifted behind me, as if restless or—

A hand descended onto my shoulder. Firm, just shy of painful in its pressure, and a few degrees colder than human.

—or as if making room for someone sneaking in.

Crap on a crispy, crumbly cracker.

"If you wouldn't mind coming with me," the owner of the hand said, voice deep and low.

"Actually, Vlad asked me to stay," I answered, trying to make eye contact with him, pleading silently.

He looked at my captor first, awe in his eyes, and I knew I was sunk. When he lowered his gaze to me, he seemed impressed. He wasn't the only one. His court had already started clearing a path. Indy and Peacock Girl both looked at me with new respect, maybe even twinged with fear.

"We can always talk later," Vlad said quickly, his failure to defend me taking him instantly from hot to *not*.

Based on the painful pressure settled on my shoulder, I wasn't so sure there'd be a later for me.

3

The vamp behind me insisted that ladies go first, steering me in front of him with that chill hand. He still hadn't allowed me to so much as turn to see who I was dealing with. This was what Sid and Maya had wanted. I was *supposed* to get caught. But plans were known to go wrong, especially around me. I tried not to let the chill creep all the way up my spine.

He led me to a dark wood door on one wall of the turret room. It looked sturdy enough that even a vamp like me might have trouble breaking it down. We were too high up for it to be a dungeon, but they probably didn't call this place the Tower for nothing. I was no history buff, but didn't people used to get walled up in towers? Wasn't that where English queens went to die when they didn't pop out baby boys? Anyway, that's how it had been in the movie I'd seen with the really awesome period clothes and jewelry and the so-stylish Anne Boleyn. It seemed old Henry the Eighth had gone through as many wives as I had shoes in my former life. Probably a slight exaggeration, but you get the biopic.

Through the door was an office, and I felt my shoulders relax just a bit at the sight. No torture devices, no armed guards. Just a plain old dark-paneled office … with no way out except for the door that shut behind us with the finality of dirt being thrown over a grave. The vamp released me and leaned against the door as an extra barrier between me and the outside world.

Now that I could, I whirled to get a decent look at my captor. *Whoa.* If Bigfoot had a nearly hairless brother, this guy was it. He had to be almost six and a half feet tall with a face overly blessed with bone and cursed with barely enough skin to cover it. Prominent brows, Jay Leno's chin, cheekbones that stuck out so far it made the rest of his face seem sunken … like Lurch from *The Addams Family.* Based on the pallor of his hair and skin, this guy hadn't seen the sun in a long, long time, which meant he was a very old vamp. Like ancient. It was no wonder Vlad had looked at him the way he did. A true believer had only to glance at Very Scary Vamp to know exactly what he was—the real deal.

Speaking of which, Very Scary crossed his arms over his chest, fixed me with his gaze, and put a considerable amount of force behind mesmerizing me with it. "Who are you?" he demanded.

As usual, the whole mesmeric magic rolled right over me.

He must have been especially strong, because I felt a tug, but it was nothing I couldn't shake off. When I'd first been vamped, a psycho-psychic told me that I was *chaos*. Maybe that was it, but if you talked to my parents, they'd tell you I'd never listened in life. Why should I be any different in death?

I hadn't expected to be captured so soon, but apparently, it was show time.

"I'm a runaway," I answered, as an opener.

Very Scary's nearly colorless brows rose to his hairline, as if he'd expected more trouble extracting information from me. "Elaborate."

"Well, okay, I haven't exactly run away *yet,* but I'm hoping you'll help me with that."

"Who are you running from and why?"

"You really don't know who I am?" I asked incredulously. "Why did you grab me then?"

He studied me, debating whether to answer. "You didn't appear on the security cameras," he said finally, moving over to the desk but keeping his gaze on me in case I made any move to escape. As if his sealed door wouldn't nip that in the bud. He opened a drawer and pressed a button hidden inside. A good quarter of the wood-paneled wall slid aside to reveal closed-circuit televisions, showing different scenes within the club. "People were reacting to and interacting with empty air. You didn't show on the video feed, but their reactions gave you away. None of my people are currently out on the floor, and I hadn't cleared anyone else for entrance. *Voilà*, intruder."

"So you came to check me out." Crud puppies—Marcy and Brent! I tried not to show my sudden concern. I had no way of getting word to them, not unless I used Bobby and his mind-speak to pass it along, but he hadn't answered me earlier. I thought fast. Maybe ... that had to be it! Giving Marcy a human partner, someone who'd show up onscreen, provided the perfect cover for people to respond in her general direction. As long as Brent stayed close there'd be no chance for anyone to put the moves on her, making their arms appear to hang in midair. I started to relax.

"May I?" I asked, gesturing toward one of the two leather-upholstered armchairs facing the desk.

"Please," he answered. He didn't sit himself, but instead perched on the edge of the desk to loom menacingly over me, arms crossed.

I took a deep breath. Out of habit, and because I was going to need it for all the explaining I had to do.

"First off, my name is Gina Covello. I'm the girl your council warned you about." If my name meant anything to him, he kept it off his face. I was a little hurt. I'd thought a Kill or Capture order from on high would make me a household name. Top of vampdom's Most Wanted; a figure to terrify the newly minted into drinking their blood like good little vamps. So much for that. "You're going to want to look me up. The fact that you've got me is going to score you a bunch of brownie points. Maybe even a reward. But it gets better. I'm here to make you a deal. I want to switch sides."

"You thought the best way to do this was to come into my club like a sneak thief and play with the humans?"

"First of all, I came in through the front door, not like a sneak thief, although I can totally rock a cat suit. Second, I wanted to get the lay of the land. You know, do some recon before presenting myself."

Very Scary Vamp opened up the long drawer of the desk, the front of which folded down so that he could access a keyboard. At the press of a button, a flat-screen rose from the desk's surface. It was wicked cool. Bobby'd be geeking out. Between that and the sliding panels hiding the security screens, I was kind of impressed myself. So weird that the public areas of the Tower were so purposely old-looking while the private parts were so high-tech modern. Apparently you *could* teach an old vamp new tricks.

He didn't explain, but I figured Very Scary was doing some recon of his own. After less than a minute he looked up, spearing me with the kind of look I'd give a pair of all-access passes for Fashion Week. He practically licked his lips.

"Now that we have you, what is it you think you can offer that's worth your freedom?"

"My boyfriend, Bobby Delvecchio, two c's. I'll wait," I said, as his fingers flew over the keyboard.

A second later, I thought I could see drool forming. While the council gave only half a damn about me, Bobby, with his major mojo, was quite the catch. "According to our files, Mr. Delvecchio is devoted to you. Why should we deal when we could as easily use you to bait a trap?"

Luckily, I had an answer for this.

"If Bobby came to my rescue—and he would—he'd burn this place to the ground. Trust me, you don't want to be on his bad side. You want him working *for* you, not against. The only way you'll get him to work for you is to let me convince him."

"Why would you do that?"

"Because you're going to make us a very attractive offer. *And* because I'm tired of having no control over my life and being locked away in a government facility between missions. No shopping, no partying. Rules, rules, rules." That last part was from the heart.

"You think working for us will grant you *more* freedom, given that we have no reason to trust you?"

I summoned my inner diva. "I think that you might be as motivated as I am to negotiate the proper incentive plan."

"I see."

Behind me came a sound, like another panel sliding aside. I couldn't help but swing around toward it, even though I didn't really want to turn my back on Very Scary. A woman and two men stood in the new doorway created, but my eyes stayed on her and her golf-pencil skirt. Ever seen a golf pencil? One-third the regular size, good for scoring. The woman exuded a sense of power the two with her lacked. Her hair was a wavy, glossy black, her skin like faded mahogany. Her nose was pierced with a very impressive diamond stud, and her eyes were ice cold and dark as obsidian.

"Selene, would you please secure our guest?" Very Scary asked. "I need to confer with the council."

"My pleasure," she answered, turning those depthless eyes on me. She had the look of a pit bull who'd just been thrown a new squeaky toy that probably wouldn't make it to dinnertime in one piece. I didn't like that comparison *at all.*

She gave a jerk of her head, and the men on either side of her flanked me, each taking an arm and "helping" me to my feet. As they held me, Selene approached to pat me down herself. She removed my rosebud, but neither man holding me used the excuse to look down my corset. I took that as a bad sign. When men are too focused to notice breasts, it's a sure signal that the crap has hit the fan.

"Let's go," she said when she concluded her search. I'd purposely come weapon-free, so there'd been nothing to find.

"I'll be in touch," Very Scary said as I was dragged along behind Selene, through the slid-back wall panel.

Next came an elevator and a ride to the basement, or what amounted to it. I thought I'd heard somewhere that there weren't a lot of basements in Florida because of the water level. Or maybe that was New Orleans. Wherever we were, Selene held her hand before a palm reader or something on the basement wall and yet another hidden door slid open before us, revealing a dungeonlike area with two cells, no windows, concrete everywhere, and a drain in the center of the floor, which I didn't even want to think about. Okay, so I was thinking about it…a drain for when they hosed the place down, right? Cleanliness, not disposal of blood and guts, surely.

These guys were really fond of their secret doors and sliding panels. If things went bad and Bobby had to rescue me…well, I might never be found.

One of Selene's goons opened a jail-like cell using a keycard attached to a cord around his waist, then saw to it that I made an entrance. Once I was in, the barred door shut behind me with a hydraulic hiss. Like the door in the boss-vamp's third floor office, I heard it auto-lock on contact.

"None of this is necessary, you know," I told her. "I came to *you*."

"So you say," Selene answered, unmoved.

"The fact that I'm here would kind of support that—"

"Selene!" a voice crackled over an intercom by the sliding panel. "Trouble out on the floor, zone 2B. Take care of it."

"Come," she ordered the two gorillas in monkey suits who'd shown me in. They followed her out.

I was left alone. All alone. Worried and wondering if Marcy was the "trouble" and whether anyone would remember about me when it all died down.

4

Sadly, this wasn't exactly my first time locked away in a dungeon. Because, oh yes, I was living *la vida loca*. Seeing the world, one dungeon at a time. Probably I could put together my own coffee table book on the subject. Or better yet, start some kind of style trend. I could see the *Project Runway* segment now—"Captive Couture, It's Killer." 'Cause nothing said style like bedpans and bindings.

It was a measure of how worried I was about Marcy that the flashbulbs in my mind quickly turned to flashfires and my quip about Bobby burning the place down around us came back to haunt me. He wouldn't really ... at least not while there were innocents around to take collateral damage. But he wasn't the only player here. What if Dion really did come back to take revenge, as the police seemed to think he might? Suddenly, it wasn't just Marcy I was worried about. It was all those other people out there in the club. And myself! Concrete might not be terribly burnable, but if the Tower went up in smoke, where would that leave me? Trapped. A tragic figure locked away like one of King Henry's wives.

Totally unacceptable.

I saw down on the end of the cot—my cell was so small, my knees practically knocked up against the bars—and closed my eyes to reach out to Bobby again. If he was listening, I knew how to get his attention.

Help, I've been deflowered! I shouted mentally, going for the psychic equivalent of an all-points bulletin.

What!!! The extra exclamation points were implied. I could almost hear his mental voice go up an octave.

My rosebud. It's gone.

Jeez, Gina, don't scare me like that.

A smile curled my lips. I couldn't help it. He was so much fun to play with. And he'd been pleasingly mesmerized by that rosebud before I left, so I was pretty sure he'd mourn the loss.

Sorry, I said, faking sincerity. *I wanted to make sure I had your attention.*

Always.

Not earlier.

Okay, always when I'm not at the bedside of a girl who's just lost her family and barely lived to tell the tale.

The little Swinter girl?

He nodded. I can't really explain it better than that. It was more a feeling of yes than the words to go with it.

She's not saying much. I don't think she considers it a victory that she's still alive, and she's going to carry those scars forever.

I couldn't even imagine. Not really. I'd lost my family when I'd been vamped, but—well, I could still see them. They just couldn't be allowed to see me. They'd been so busy jet-setting even before my "death" that the difference barely registered. Really.

Scars? I asked.

Emotional and physical. Someone chowed down on her. The marks resemble vampire bites, but ... these aren't going to heal like the real thing. They're going to be a constant reminder of the attack.

Poor kid, I answered. The need to fake sincerity had fallen straight away. I tried to imagine what the girl was going through and couldn't. *Did she tell you anything helpful?*

She didn't *say her sister was involved.*

But you think she might be? I interpreted.

It's all in her silences. Bobby fell silent himself for a second, as if some kind of emergency broadcast was interrupting his signal.

Bobby? I called.

Where are you? he asked, sounding suddenly urgent.

Well, that's what I was calling to tell you ...

Marcy says she and Brent lost sight of you a while ago and now there's a raid—

Police raid?

He agreed, and I breathed a sigh of relief. Not fire, then ... or psycho killer. Anything else, Marcy and Brent should be able to handle. The Feds had cleared the agency's involvement with the locals, but blowing cover wasn't exactly in our mission statement. Marcy and Brent's IDs ought to hold. If you couldn't count on the Feds to forge decent documents, who could you trust?

So, you're where? he prompted

Sticking to the plan, I promised. *I've laid out our proposition. They've, ah, locked me up. Just 'til they can check me out,* I assured him. *But in case there's any problem I wanted to let you know they've got me stuck in some dungeony room inside the Tower.* I did my best to send him a mental map.

Got it. Stay safe, he ordered.

I debated how many fingers to use in my salute. I wasn't so good at taking orders, even the semi-sweet, overprotective, macho-boyfriend type. My parents had been pretty hands-off. The Feds only cared about me as an investment they wanted to mature. To have someone *actually* care ... I still hadn't figured out quite how to react.

I heard a sound then and froze, trying to determine if it was in or outside of my head. There was a follow-up click-click. Out. Definitely out.

I sent Bobby a quick *Gotta go* and started as I met the unblinking gaze of an eye-level Selene. She'd squatted to facilitate the face-to-face, somehow managing not to pull a Lindsay Lohan in her teeny tiny skirt. She smiled at my reaction. Not that it reached those cold, moonless-midnight eyes; the faux vampiress at the Tower door had it all wrong with her kitty-cat contacts. I wondered if my own eyes would go as dark and dim as Selene's after long enough of been there, bitten that, have the bloody T-shirt to prove it. Unh uh. No flippin' way. I had a lot of life in me yet. Just, you know, not literally.

After what I'd heard from Bobby, I didn't have a lot of patience for games. "You gonna kiss me or kill me?" I asked.

She was highly unimpressed by my bravado. "Tell me about the proposal you made to Lucas," she ordered. She didn't bother to put any *oomph* behind it. Not that it would have worked on me, but usually vamps tried. They couldn't help themselves. Ms. Mini-skirt seemed to count on her intimidating display of legs and her winning personality to get me to talk.

"If you tell *me* what the trouble was upstairs," I answered, since I wasn't supposed to know and was curious, anyway, about *why* the police had raided.

"I'll ask the questions," she stated, her voice as flat as her eyes. I determined right then to get a rise out of her. Maybe not the healthiest decision I'd ever made, but what good was eternal life if you didn't live a little?

"Sure," I answered agreeably. "Ask away."

"Tell me all about it. The Truth." She spoke in capitals. You could just hear it.

I blinked, and took a few unnecessary breaths just to mark the passing of time before breaking eye contact to study my nails. In case you're wondering whether nails grow after death—

Selene growled. Low, like a junkyard dog with the teeth to back up the threat, not the loud rumble of a big, bad bluff.

I looked up and met her gaze again. "Oh, you want me to *answer*," I said, feigning surprise. "Well, then, how about a little tit for tat? As I told Very Scary up there, I plan to become a valuable resource. A little respect would be nice."

"Respect is earned."

"Yeah, I read that in a fortune cookie once. So go ahead, start earning."

Oh, her eyes sparked now. "You do know the order out on you is *Kill* or Capture, right? I don't think the council's terribly picky about how many pieces you come in."

"No, but I'm worth more as a set."

She seemed to take that in as a breath and rose again to her full height as she rolled it around on her tongue like I'd seen my father do with a wine he'd chosen with dinner. An actual expression threatened to mar the Ice Queen of the Damned thing she had going on, and it was … confusion? Surprise? She covered it quickly, but—

"Tell me more about that."

"About Bobby? Geez, I'd think you guys would have a dossier by now. He's my sire and we're pretty much like this." I put my middle finger over my index to show how tight we were—at least when we could find a deserted hallway or a free second at spook central. That boy could *kiss.* "The deal is: you make us a sweet offer, we'll take you up on it."

Selene was carefully trying for blank, but not quite achieving it. If I had to guess at the look, I'd peg it as frustration. "Say that again."

I looked at her funny. Something was wrong. Yet I had a strange feeling it wasn't my problem.

"Make us a sweet offer," I repeated, "and we're all yours."

Her look didn't clear. If anything, it was deeper, darker, brows lowered like she was trying to puzzle something out.

It came to me in a flash. "You're a truth-teller!" I blurted.

I'd read about them in the Federal files. You'd think homework would end with death, but you'd be wrong. College or spy school, it was all the same, though the exams tended to be a little more intense when your life depended on passing. Speaking of the spooks, Sid and Maya would give the sticks up their butts to learn about Selene. Truth-tellers were legendary. As in literally the stuff of legends. None seen for, like, decades.

She didn't answer, but on a gut level I knew I was right. Points to me. For figuring it out *and* for being totally—what was the word?—*inscrutable.* I wasn't sure I had that right. Could someone be *in*scrutable when they couldn't be *scrutable* to begin with? I'd have to ask Bobby.

I somehow didn't think Selene would tell me. Right now, her lips were smooshed like two slices of bread in a panini press.

A victory dance probably wasn't a sound survival strategy.

"Look, I have all night, apparently," I said, glancing pointedly at the dungeon walls. "But I can think of better ways to spend it. So why don't we cut to the chase? You want what I have but you don't trust me yet to get it for you. Tell me how to change that."

She eyed me coldly. "For one, if we let you out, you will not speculate to your federal friends about my supposed abilities. I don't think true death would become you."

Oh no, she did not just threaten my life *and* tell me I'd make an ugly corpse.

"Of course," I answered with false sweetness. "Your secret's safe with me."

"Next, you are here to find Nelson Ricci, yes? The bloody boy who goes by *Dion*?"

I was so surprised at how well-informed she was that I just stared. I was supposed to win her trust. It certainly made things easier on me if I could do that by telling her something she already knew. "How did you—?"

"When you find him, you will bring him to *us*."

My brain fell all over itself trying to figure that one out. He was a *boy*. A sociopathic boy to be sure, but still. What could the vamps want with him? Maybe to pin a medal on his chest for cutting his fellow humans down to size, evening out the vamp-to-human ratio one kill at a time? But in the grand scheme of things...

"Why?" I asked. "I mean, I don't care who has him, but why would you want him?" For that matter, what had the Feds so interested? His crimes were horrible, of course, but federal? I wasn't so sure.

"I don't see that it's any business of yours."

"I've never been good with 'just do as you're told,'" I said honestly. "I'm looking for *more* freedom, not less." I gave her my most unblinking stare.

"Right now, you're a mere foot soldier. You follow orders, no questions asked. When—if—you work your way up to General, you'll have all the freedom you could want."

Military analogies—really?

"Fine, I'll bring you the head of Nelson Ricci."

"Alive," she said.

I huffed. "I never said the rest of his body wouldn't be attached. So, Nelson Ricci. Anything else I can get for you? Chill pill? Breath mint?"

Selene growled again, but deep down I suspected I was growing on her.

"Screw orders," she mumbled. "I bet you'd snap like a

twig." But then she got herself under control. "I'll send some-one to let you out."

She whirled gracefully for the door and marched her-self out. A second later, I was alone with nothing but time to think.

That was when I realized that Selene had never answered my questions. I'd been so caught up in my victory over her mental mojo that I hadn't noticed. Apparently, truth-telling wasn't her only interrogational skill. Her evasion topped the charts. Something else occurred to me as well—Selene could have let me out herself as easily as arranging to have it done. I'd figured it was a power thing, like "I'm too high and mighty for manual labor," but what if there was more to it? Thinking back, I realized I'd never seen Selene touch a thing. Not the panels that slid out of her way, the bars of my prison or, heaven forbid, *me*. Yet the *snap me like a twig* comment led me to believe she *could* grab me if she wanted to. So why? My mind boggled. A vampire germaphobe? Silly but not impossible. If personalities survived death, why not phobias? Or maybe, hav-ing a legendary power herself, she was truly paranoid of other potential powers, like telemetry. I'd learned about that in the same file where I'd read about truth-telling. It was the power to read the history of a person, place, or thing by touching it. Maybe she didn't want to leave any kind of trace. Or maybe I was making magic out of molehills.

•   •   •

We need to talk, I thought at Bobby as I left the Tower, the tiny Batphone the vamps had given me for making contact tucked down into my cleavage.

There was a momentary delay, during which I was sure he wasn't listening, and then he answered distractedly, *Meet you back at base.*

Not there.

I could feel his surprise and his sudden full attention. *What's up?*

As far as I knew, the Feds still hadn't learned to eavesdrop on mental speak, but it was hard to figure what to say when I hardly knew myself what I was thinking. Both the Feds and the vamps were hiding something, I was sure, but what? It might be more secure talking to Bobby in mind-speak, but some things, like potential conspiracies, took hashing out in person. Anyway, if the Tampa vamps had eyes on me, it would help my story to be seen luring Bobby away from our handlers for some private conversation, as long as they kept to their agreement to let me bring him in willingly.

I don't know exactly what's up, but ... I think maybe we should put our heads together and figure it out.

Huh?

I stood just outside the club exit, a little apart from the smokers. Clearly the police raid hadn't scared everyone off. In fact, on my way out of the Tower, escorted by Selene's goon squad, I didn't notice much thinning of the crowd from earlier. It could be that raids only added to the mystique of the place.

I looked around for somewhere to ask Bobby to meet me—a late-night coffee shop or something—but I was back in the alleyway I'd entered from and there was nothing to be seen but the back end of other warehousey businesses. Very scenic.

The club door opened behind me. *We'll talk later,* I told Bobby, turning with the expectation of trouble.

Framed in the doorway, the backlighting turning his sandy brown hair an antique gold, was the Indiana Jones of the Burgess Brigade.

He slipped out, closing the door behind him, killing the glow. I stepped aside to give him room to pass, but he moved right along with me, his eyes meeting mine and holding in a way that said we weren't meeting in a dark alley by accident. If I'd thought about his eyes at all, it was with the expectation that they'd be brown like the rest of him, but instead they were a deep moss green.

"Cosette?" he asked.

"Yes, and you are?"

"Hunter." He gave a courtly kind of bow that I could get used to. Men didn't exactly bow down before me on a daily basis, something I considered a cosmic injustice.

"You want something?" I asked, cautious despite the bow. I'd gotten in with the true vamps just as I was supposed to, but I hadn't forgotten that there were *humans* behind the violence I'd seen in the Feds' photos. Even if he'd been exiled, Dion had been one of the lifestylers and might still have allies among them. Hunter could very well be one of the unidentified shadows from the film.

"Walk with me?" he asked.

"Why not." It wasn't like I couldn't take him … in a fair fight.

Pleased, Hunter raised a hand as if to put it to my back, to guide me out of the alley, but then hesitated and dropped it without making contact. Somehow, I managed to turn all on my own and make it to the street.

"Where to?" I asked. Maybe I could find a good place for Bobby and me to meet during the walk.

"This way," he answered, and started toward the left, in the direction that seemed darker and less likely to lead to any other signs of late-night civilization. If I weren't a vamp, I might be worried.

We walked in silence for half a minute, which was about all I could take. "Just spill," I told him.

"Excuse me?"

"You asked me to walk with you for a reason, and you haven't once gawked at my legs"—flashing with every step because of the hip-high slits—"so I know that's not it. There's something else you want."

He slid a look at my legs now that I'd pointed them out, and an appreciative smile lit his face. "Hold on a second. I might just have to revise my priorities."

"Down boy," I ordered. Because, for one, while he was easy on the eyes, he was also, like, *old*. Maybe even thirty. For another, I was taken.

He sighed and stopped walking, turning to study me with a near-religious intensity. Those moss-green eyes did *intensity* really well.

"You're one of them, aren't you?" he asked finally.

"One of who?"

"*Them*."

Clear as mud.

"Look, if that's what this is all about, we can turn around right now." I started to do that very thing.

"Hear me out," he insisted, putting a hand on my arm to stop me. I glanced at the hand until he regained his senses and removed it. "Look, I've read Rachel Caine and Faith Hunter and all that. I know about human servants. I want to offer myself."

I blinked. Since he thought of me as some higher life form, I didn't want to blurt out "Huh?" and ruin the whole thing, but it was right on the tip of my tongue.

"You need a daysider, right?" he rushed on, probably seeing my lack of on-boardness. "I noticed you don't have anyone with you. No entourage or anything. I figured you might be new and that I could—"

"Stop." I held up a hand to reinforce the command, and he paused like I'd hit a button on the universal remote. I had to process this. Nothing in the Federal files had talked about human servants. I mean, yeah, the vampire vixen that Bobby and I'd escaped from when we'd first risen had employed humans to work for her, and sometimes she used her mental mojo to assure obedience, but they weren't exactly her servants. I didn't know what all they got out of the arrangement, except probably a salary and the hope of becoming one of us with good behavior.

I *had* always wanted an entourage, but I didn't see how it would fit in with my super-secret life. Plus, I couldn't imagine Bobby'd be too happy with "He followed me home, can I keep him?"

"I understand; you've only just met me," Hunter continued, apparently unable to hold his silence. "Let me prove to you how useful I can be."

Something moved in the shadows. "Let's walk," I said abruptly, suddenly on high alert. The vamps wanted something from me I hadn't yet delivered, so whatever I'd seen—too big to be an alley cat—had to be human. No problem. Unless, of course, they were armed with pointy sticks, garlic, and holy water. Doubtful, but hey, if people could go around thinking they were vampires or the second coming of Charles Mad-eye Manson, like Dion did, then others could surely believe themselves vampire hunters. Without stakes, whatever stalked us didn't stand a chance against me, but I wasn't exactly cruising for a fight. I might break a newly polished nail.

"But … " Hunter planted himself there on the sidewalk, apparently prepared not to move until I agreed to his request, and oblivious to the threat near us. At that very moment, the shadow I'd seen materialized into a man.

"You should have listened to the lady," he said, voice emerging from the depths of his black hoodie, which was just so, so *cliché* that I didn't even have words. He held an open flip knife beside his thigh, a subtle but clear threat. "Isn't that right, B?"

I turned my head, trying to keep my body between Hunter and the blade—the one I knew of, anyway—and saw a second shadow step out of an alleyway on the other side of us. Same black hoodie, but with a flicker of metal at the neckline. I was too taken with the sparkly he held at his hip—all gleaming death—to pay proper attention to his bling. This was no flip knife, which was deadly enough, but a big, bad blade with barbs as it approached the handle. It would cut you like butter going in and tear through you like trans fat on the way out.

"Oh crap," Hunter said, summing things up nicely.

"Stay behind me," I ordered.

"How?" he asked.

He had a point. I only had one backside, and there were two toughs.

"Hand over your wallets," the first hooded horror demanded.

I didn't have a wallet so much as a slim card case dangling from my wrist with my ID, plastic, and a little cold hard cash. If I were all by my lonesome, I'd kick hoodlum heinie and hold onto my valuables. I was pretty sure getting jacked of my ID the first night of the mission would lose me serious spook cred. But with Hunter to worry about…

Slowly, so as not to worry the bladed baddies, I slid the strap of my card case off my wrist. Hunter, unfortunately, was not so smart.

"You can take 'em," he hissed. "Why are you holding back?"

Sensing they were losing us, "B" moved in with his monster blade and instinct took over. I got a stranglehold on my wrist strap and swung the card case like a nunchuk, bringing it crashing down on B's hand with vampire force. His knuckles cracked, and he howled loudly enough that company would be only a matter of time. The knife clattered to the sidewalk and I kicked it aside. It went skittering into the night, outside the corona of the streetlights.

"Cosette!" Hunter yelled.

I turned in time to see his eyes go wide as Flip-knife jammed his weapon into Hunter's side. Swinging my makeshift sap again, I let out some warrior princess–sounding battle cry and went for the bladed baddie. He yanked his knife out, letting Hunter slide to the ground as he turned to face me.

B lunged at me from behind, grabbing me by the corset

strings with his good hand, holding me in place while his partner closed on me. If I ripped free, I wondered what would give first—B's fingers or my laces. I didn't want to be flapping in the breeze, but it would make a hell of a distraction.

I stomped down on B's instep, did the classic elbow-to-the-stomach, then hurled him over my shoulder when he doubled over in pain. He choked out a cry like a wounded wildebeest. His partner barely had time to point the knife away before B's body was somersaulting through the air, hitting the ground hard and rolling into his friend, feet flailing straight to the gut.

The air whooshed out of Flip-knife's lungs, but he kept control of his blade and clumsily vaulted his friend to get to me.

"You bitch!" he screamed.

"Be-yotch, please," I told him. "Show some respect."

He growled and dove with the knife, too angry for finesse. I blocked the blade with a swing of my crackin' card case and countered with a two-fingered blow to the soft spot on the neck. He fell gurgling to his knees, knife finally dropping to the pavement. I'd stopped short of using enough force to crush his windpipe. He'd live, but he wouldn't be too happy about it for awhile.

There was yelling from down the street. As glad as I was that help was on the way for the wounded, I didn't want to get tied up giving witness.

Quickly, I knelt by Hunter's side to check on him. It was a good sign that his eyes were wide open and tracking.

"*That* was *awesome*," he whispered.

I ignored that and felt for the wound on his side. I was

no expert, but it didn't seem to be anywhere vital. He was lucky it had been the flip knife and not the monster blade that pierced him. The smell of blood was making me crazy. I'd exerted a lot of energy. I was *hungry*, and Hunter smelled really, really good. Not mochachino good, but almost. My teeth lengthened. I hurriedly patted him down for ID so I could look in on him later.

"Police!" someone called. "Stop right there."

I tucked the business card I'd found into my cleavage and whispered "Not a word" in Hunter's ear. I threw whatever mesmeric mojo I might have behind it.

Then I was off into the night, still safe with my secret identity. If there was any pursuit, it never even came close as I circled back to the club for my car.

5

I met up with Bobby at a hookah place he'd found that was open late. I had no idea what a hookah was until I stepped inside the smoky bar, which was apparently exempt from the indoor smoking laws, and found groups of people looking like the caterpillar from *Alice in Wonderland*, inhaling scented smoke through long tubes extending like tentacles from a central, lamplike pipe. I figured it was a really good thing I didn't have to breathe.

Bobby waved to me from a dark corner, no problem at all to spot with my vamp-o-vision. He had one of those crazy contraptions in front of him for cover and even seemed to be taking hits off it. My nose crinkled.

"What?" he asked. "It's not like we can get lung cancer or anything."

"No, but stinky clothes and stained teeth are just as deadly to your social life."

"So I'll shower and brush. Want to try? It's cherry flavored."

That did sound almost tempting. Since I'd been vamped, I hadn't been able to eat or drink anything but blood. The one time my friends and I had tried, we almost got to see ourselves from the inside out. My stomach still ached to think of it. So the idea of flavor, any way I could get it, was ... irresistible.

"Gimme."

Bobby handed me the tube he'd been using and I put it to my lips. I took a deep breath—

And launched into a five-minute coughing fit. The smoke burned like someone had shot shards of glass straight into my lungs.

Around me there were low chuckles, some head-shaking, and stares.

"It's an acquired taste," Bobby said, trying to bury his own smile.

I handed the tube back. "No thanks. You acquire it then."

He smiled. "So glad I have your permission. Anyway, I can't see making a habit of it, but maybe once in a while ... " He got this wistful look in his eyes, and I knew he was think- ing about flavor as well. If they had a mochachino or dulce de leche option, I might have had to reconsider, but ...

"Good, because I have to admit, the whole fire and brim- stone thing—so not a turn on," I said.

"Ever been kissed by a smoker?" he asked, leaning toward me. "Makes your lips tingle."

"Oh yeah?" I asked, leaning in myself to meet him half-way. "Prove it."

He did, grabbing the back of my neck and brushing his lips across mine, gently at first, only feather-light. My lips opened beneath his. I definitely felt a tingling, but I didn't think it had anything to do with tobacco. And then he moved in for more—a devouring kiss. Any last bit of breath I had sighed out when his tongue slid into my mouth, hot and intimate. I grabbed his shoulders to hold him in place and kissed him back, our tongues dueling, the zing starting to spread throughout my whole body.

A throat cleared to my right, and as tempted as I was to ignore it, Bobby pulled back. I turned with a glare.

"Can I get the lady anything?" the server asked pointedly.

"The lady is just fine, thank you," I answered, knowing full well the interruption had been more about, well, *interrupting* than service. The man went off in a huff.

"I think that was the polite form of 'get a room,'" Bobby said.

"Sounds good to me."

His smile matched mine. "First things first. You wanted to talk?"

My smile faded. "Oh, yeah." I paused for a second, wondering how to put all my doubts into words. "This mission … something's not right."

"How do you mean?"

"Well, for one, this case—I know the Feds want to get you and me in with the vamps as double agents, but they could do that anywhere, any time. Why fly us all the way out to Florida? Why this elaborate scheme? I mean, the murders are really awful and all, but they don't cross state lines or involve terrorism or anything. They might be the start of a series, but we don't even know that yet. And why commit two whole agents, Marcy and Brent, to investigating the humans? Plus, you on background checks. That's three quarters of our team. There's got to be more here than they're telling us."

"Maybe the case was just in a convenient time and place. The Feds could kill two birds with one stone—take out vamps and killers alike."

"That's what I thought—until tonight. The vamps are interested in Dion, too. And not just to terminate him for smearing the good name they don't have since they're still hush-hush and all. They want him alive."

Bobby thought about that for a minute. "Maybe they want their own kind of private justice."

"You think so?"

"No. I don't think they'd waste that kind of time on a mere human, especially one who others are looking to take care of anyway. But it's a possibility."

"Okay, fine, it's a possibility. I'm still going to look into the alternatives."

"Like what?"

"I don't know yet. It just feels all wrong. You know, women's intuition or whatever. We have to investigate."

Bobby didn't look convinced.

I huffed. "What do you think is more likely—that the spy guys are telling us everything, or that we're on a need-to-know basis?"

"That last part," he admitted.

"Right, well, *I* need to know the whole story, don't you? What if there's something important they're hiding?"

"Like what?"

"If I knew that, it wouldn't be *hidden*, right?"

"R-i-ight."

"Okay, so we investigate."

"We spy on the spies?" Bobby asked dubiously.

"Well … yeah. I mean, it's what they want me to do anyway. I'm supposed to pretend to the fangs that I'm a double agent. Might as well play it up."

"What if we get caught?"

I pulled away from him and studied those seriously blue eyes. "Are you telling me you're afraid of *Sid*?"

His eyes crinkled up at the corners in a way I loved and that his vamp mojo would never let develop into wrinkles. Win-win.

"No," he answered.

"Good, because brainy boys with balls—totally sexy."

"Really?"

The waiter came back again to slam the check down on the table in front of us before Bobby and I could go in for another kiss. He cleared his throat meaningfully when neither of us moved quickly enough to pay up and get out.

"You ought to get that looked at," Bobby said as he threw down a bill on top of the check. "Sounds like you're coming down with something."

The server sneered and walked off. I hadn't paid any attention to the bill Bobby'd thrown down. I wasn't sure he had either. But I hoped it didn't include a big tip, since the waiter never even asked if he wanted change.

"So, where do we start?" Bobby asked me.

Spying on the Feds had seemed like a good idea when it was still theoretical, but my stomach was now starting to jitterbug like the time I downed a whole twenty-ounce bottle of Jolt while studying for finals.

We rose from our seats, and I leaned over to breathe in Bobby's ear, "Well, it's a little late to start tonight. Maybe we can go back to the privacy of my place and discuss this further."

Bobby smoothed my hair back from my ear, causing a delicious shiver all the way through me. "What kind of *discussion* did you have in mind?" he breathed back.

"The non-verbal kind," I said.

The gleam in his eyes said he liked that thought—a lot.

He held me as we walked out to our cars, as if we were some normal couple out on a date. It was nice. Really nice.

"I'll follow you," he said as we got to my car, giving me a squeeze before letting me go.

I watched him as he walked to his own vehicle, because he looked just as good going as coming. It's a tragic fact that some guys are born totally without butt. Bobby was not one of them. His butt very nicely filled out his slacks, which looked tailored to him. Totally grabbable.

I sighed. Bobby looked back over his shoulder and caught me staring. I stuck out my tongue at him and he licked his lips. Fire sped through my body. "Hurry," I said. I almost didn't even want to kick him for the smug smile he sent back, as if he could read my mind. Hell, he probably could.

I turned to my car before I could be any more stupidly

vulnerable, clicked it open, and checked inside like I'd been taught to be sure no one was waiting in ambush. Then I slid into the driver's seat. I made sure Bobby was behind me before peeling out of the parking lot. Way conscious of my dignity, I *wo*manfully resisted breaking all land-speed records to get home.

I was leaning, pin-up girl style, against my bumper when Bobby pulled into the parking lot of my apartment building.

"What took you so long?" I asked in my sultriest voice.

"Actually stopping for that red light back there," he answered.

Okay, so I'd had only moderate success on the whole land-speed thing.

"Sorry, it was yellow when I went through."

"Maybe for the first millimeter of your bumper—"

I bucked myself away from my car and stepped up to him, sliding my hands over his chest. "Is this really what you want to use that mouth for?"

His eyes glazed over, I swear it. He took a deep breath and said, nearly on a sigh, "No."

"Good." I took his hand and led him to my place—second floor rear in an apartment block with four units. The few times I'd been here—to sign the lease and to move in "Gail Kuttner's" few belongings—the cocker spaniel next door had gone nuts, barking up a storm as I approached like some kind of mutt motion detector. Tonight his owner must have had him out on a walk, because all was mercifully silent as we reached my apartment.

Bobby slid his arms around me from behind and nipped my neck as I unlocked the door. We didn't really need lights, so

I didn't turn them on as we entered, though I did twirl out of Bobby's hold long enough to shut and lock the door behind us.

Bobby backed me up against it and continued his attention to my neck, licking and nipping, though not drawing blood, not sinking his fangs in, as I wanted him to so badly. My own fangs slid down, fully extended, and I didn't know how Bobby resisted. I wanted to taste him. His shirt was a button-up, probably so he'd look all official hanging out with the other Feds. I made short work of the buttons and peeled the tailored shirt off his body. Bobby let go of me long enough for me to slip it off his arms. A bare-chested Bobby was a beautiful thing, and I pushed him back to have a look at him. He was more swimmer-lean than body-builder bulky, but the kind of swimmer who did a lot of, I don't know, breast stroke or something, because his pecs were *very* well developed, and his stomach was washboard.

"Couch," I ordered.

Bobby grinned, saluted, and turned—at which point, the grin died a horrible and too-sudden death. I followed his gaze, and all that lovely heat fled my body in a rush.

SORRY WE MISSED YOU.

It was painted on the wall directly over the couch. Big, bold, red letters.

"Is that ... blood?" I asked faintly.

Then I realized how stupid that was. If I hadn't been so overwhelmed with Bobby when we came in, I would have noticed it right away, as I did now—the smell of fresh paint.

"Nevermind," I murmured.

Bobby's eyes blazed as he turned back to me. "I'll check the rest of the apartment. You call it in."

I nodded, too stunned to protest Bobby putting himself in charge. And besides, the macho-protective thing was maybe just a little bit sexy—not that I'd ever admit it or anything. I dialed Maya, listed as "Mom" in my directory. She answered on the second ring.

"The killer kids," I said without even a greeting. "I think they came for me. Bobby's checking the apartment over now."

"Clear," he called from the bedroom.

"He says it's clear, but they left a message on the wall." I paused as she asked a question. "No, this one's in paint. I guess with no victim they didn't have a handy source of blood other than their own. CSI shows have probably convinced them that's not the way to go ... Right, thanks."

I hit the *End* button and started to collapse onto the couch, but Bobby yelled "Stop!" from the bedroom doorway. When I froze halfway down, in an awkward hovering position, he added, "Check it first. Just in case it's booby-trapped."

"Wow, paranoid much?" I asked. Only the paranoia was as contagious as a yawn. Now that he'd put it into my head, I had to check.

Nervously, I patted down the cushions to be sure none were primed with spring-loaded stakes or other craziness. Pain burst over my hands like a flashfire.

I shrieked and drew back my smoking hands, the flesh charred where I'd brushed the couch. I blew on my fingers and palms, as if it would help, but even the gentle breeze blazed like hellfire.

Bobby grabbed me by the shoulders and raced me to the kitchen sink. He turned on the cold water and held my hands under the stream. Far too slowly, the pain downgraded from kill-me-now to sitting-through-*Van Helsing.* My fingers throbbed with an almost unbearable pain, and I was afraid to look at the damage.

"How bad?" I asked Bobby, my eyes squinched shut.

"You'll heal," he said softly, but I could tell it was bad. "They must have sprinkled holy water over the couch."

"You think?" I asked. I didn't mean to be snarky, but screaming pain will do that to a girl. "There's bottled blood in the fridge," I told him. "Maybe—"

But he was shaking his head. "I wouldn't trust it. Could be tainted. In fact, I wouldn't stay here tonight. There's no telling what else they've rigged, and once the sun rises—"

I'd be completely vulnerable. Oh, the Feds had a formula that would let us operate by day, but the vamps knew all about it—thanks to my ex-minion, Rick, who turned ratfink on our last mission. Since this assignment catered to our night sides, no one was willing to give the formula to us now. It wasn't worth the risk that it might fall into the wrong hands.

"What I don't understand," Bobby went on, "is how they found you so fast. And why."

"I don't *know*," I said, trying not to sound as pitiful as I felt at that moment. I only wanted to collapse onto something and coddle my poor hands, but I didn't trust anything enough to relax. "I only showed my ID to one person tonight. The girl taking the cover charge at the Tower door, but—"

Bobby whipped out his cell phone before I could finish. My fingers strobed, as if with sympathy pain, with every button he pressed. My raw nerves felt like guitar strings being plucked by some overeager beginner. Even my *nails* hurt, my manicure marred with heat blisters and boiled to black.

He was busy telling whoever was on the other end of the line about the girl, when suddenly he stopped and held the phone out to me, up to my ear so I didn't have to touch it myself. "Describe her," he ordered.

So I did, cat's-eye contacts and all, not that *that* would be any help. She probably didn't wear them around out in the real world. I hadn't noticed the height of her heels—clearly I was slipping—so I couldn't even give them a sense of stature. Her size was easy, though. A four. Maybe a six, tops.

Bobby took the phone back and listened for a sec before adding, "Oh, and hey, bring blood."

I was so meltingly grateful that I almost didn't call him on the bossy thing. "But you never let me finish," I accused as he disconnected. "The girl could have told anyone who I was, if she even bothered to notice. Though there was no reason why she would have. Heck, she scanned my ID—anyone associated with the club could have gotten my home address."

"Those machines don't record the IDs, they just shine a kind of light on them that lets whoever's looking detect tampering."

"As far as you know. I mean, look, we didn't even know about vampires before we woke up dead, or about the juju brigade before we got recruited."

"Now who's paranoid?"

"Gah, men!"

He smiled, and even though it should have been obnoxious, it kind of went straight to my heart. I know, right? Stupid. Still . . . sucker punch.

"Okay, we'll call scanning a possibility," Bobby agreed. "I still say the girl herself is a good place to start. As you said, it was clearly someone associated with the club."

"Someone who knew or guessed I was a vampire."

"Maybe. We don't actually know until the team does their sweep. Maybe the would-be killers were hedging their bets. Could be they've set human booby traps as well. I didn't spring anything, but I was only looking to be sure they'd vacated the place. I wasn't looking for hidden death."

"But why come after me at all?"

"Why go after the Swinter family? I'm not sure we're talking about motives that would make sense to you and me. If this is a cult, like a Manson family sort of thing... killing might be its own reward."

I shuddered. "Lovely."

Bobby pulled me into a very gentle hug, and I held my hands loosely at my sides so they wouldn't get bumped. He was solid and sexy, and if I wasn't very careful, I'd forget everything my momma ever taught me and fall head over heels in love. I'd already let him live after he'd turned me to the dark side, which, contrary to popular belief, didn't even have cookies. Worse, he'd gotten me recruited as a super spy, though that last wasn't *entirely* his fault.

"Think of it this way," he said, stroking my hair in such a way that if I were a cat, I would have purred. "The next best thing to knowing where Dion and his crew *are* is to know where they will be. 'Sorry we missed you' sounds like they'll be back."

That moved me off my warm fuzzy thoughts but quick. "Great. So once again I'm supposed to be the Nightcrawler of the Damned."

"Nightcrawler?"

"Sure. Aren't they used as bait?"

6

No one expected the baddies to be back that night or the crime-scene techs to be finished with my place before dawn, plus the Feds wanted to go over our cars with a fine-toothed comb, so Bobby and I got a chauffeured ride to the pawnshop—meaning, the local front for the Feds that we'd turned into our temporary headquarters. It seemed an odd choice of location until I realized that, aside from Disney and Universal, any building in Florida that wasn't medi-cal—clinic, wellness center, hospital, or health insurance—was a pawnshop, bail bonds office, or guns-and-ammo place. Nothing could be more common or less remarkable. Apparently, everyone in Florida was either dyin' or tryin'.

By the time we got to the spy shop and Bobby had made

his bad joke about us all being pawns in the grand chess game of life, it was nearly dawn and I was done in. But neither impending sun nor sleep were allowed to keep us from a debriefing. Bobby and I were ushered into a small conference room in the back with black-out shades, probably covering bricked-up or sound-proofed windows that protected against noise transmitting to any directional microphones that might be aimed our way.

I collapsed into one of the chairs at the conference table, my skirt falling away to reveal scads of thigh. Agent Stuffed Shirt—Sid—looked away quickly, which made me grin. I didn't exactly *live* to discomfort him; I thought of it more as a death benefit.

What he looked away *to* was an off-center image of Brent up on a flat-panel TV screen. I looked at Bobby. "Webcam," he whispered. "Fairly high res."

I assumed the last part was geek-speak and moved right along, focusing on what Brent had to report.

"—closed the place down around two," Brent was saying, "but we got invited to the after-party in some artist-space downtown. You know, the kind with lots of small studios. Their unit was like an underground movie house. Huge projector screen, lots of couches ... "

"*All* of them in use," Marcy chimed in, and I realized that was why Brent was off-center. He'd made room on camera for Marcy, even though her image wouldn't get picked up. For some reason, we vamps screwed with visuals but not audio. Totally wrecked my childhood dream of rocking runways from New York to Milan.

"Marcy!" I called. I couldn't help it. I was so glad to hear her voice.

"Gina! You're okay!"

"They didn't tell you?" I asked, turning on Sid.

"Calm down," he ordered. "We hadn't gotten there yet." To Brent: "The warehouse—you have the address?"

"Yeah, I've already texted you the information. I'm scanning the cards we got and sending the info from Marcy's arms as well."

"Her arms?" Sid asked.

"Yeah, she was a big hit with the Steampunk crowd. She got a bunch of phone numbers."

"Penny Dreadful is going to help me make my own doomsday dress!" Marcy cut in excitedly.

"Lucky!" I called.

"I know, right? Those costumes are wicked."

"Focus," Sid growled. "What did you learn?"

It was Brent who answered. "We have a last-known address on Dion, but word is he's moved on, and we've got the names of three other kids who were disillusioned with the vampire scene. They checked out around the same time as Dion."

"Good work," Sid said.

Dawn was pulling at my eyelids, making my whole body feel heavy. If we didn't wrap this up soon—

"One more thing," Brent added. "The older Swinter girl, the one who's disappeared—she was part of the scene. They say Dion followed her around like a puppy until a week or so before he got booted, when he went off the grid for a few days. He was so changed when he came back, spouting so many crazy-dangerous ideas, that the Burgess Brigade petitioned for his exile."

"What kind of ideas?" Sid asked.

My head hit the table, too heavy to hold up any more. I heard Bobby's thunk down as well. The room grew dark. And then … nothingness.

• • •

I fell awake. I know, the expression is "fell asleep," but trust me on this. You know that sense of falling into a bottomless pit where your hands and feet lash out trying to find something to stop the descent, and you bolt awake clutching the covers? Your head pounds, sweat beads at your temples, and your mind is certain you've just narrowly dodged death, all evidence to the contrary. *That* was how it felt to wake when the sun set. Put another way, it was like someone used those medical paddles to zap me back from the brink of death to the land of the living. Except that my heart still didn't beat. I'd have fallen out of my chair if I'd still been back in the conference room, but someone had moved me to a room with no view and thrown a blanket over me.

"Hey," said Bobby, from the other cot in the tiny room, "anyone ever tell you you're beautiful in the evening?"

I smiled over at him—so cute, even with his bed head. "Yes, but I don't mind hearing it again."

"Well, then—"

The door burst open, revealing Sid as serious as I'd ever seen him, and that was saying something. A vein jumped along his jaw, which was set tight. That jaw seemed not so much to move as to break away from the rest of his face when he said,

"Good, you're up. Conference room *now*. We've had another incident." He vanished again.

Bobby and I looked at each other and scrambled to follow. Let me tell you—corsets, for all their fashion do's, are a serious action *don't*. It was physically impossible to rise quickly in a corset without breaking something... like a rib.

Still, we managed to make it to the conference room before Sid sent out a search party.

"Don't suppose you've got the blood of a caffeine addict on tap?" I asked, as I sank back into my chair from yesterday.

Then the image on the big-screen, the one Brent had spoken to us from the night before, caught my eye. What it showed shut me right up. I recognized that industrial gray carpeting... and those legs, with the baggy old-lady stockings constantly slipping down around the ankles beneath her house dress. I let out a cry.

Even with the rest of her mercifully hidden behind the couch, I could tell that my nice neighbor lady with the spaniel was dead.

Bobby reached over to take my hand. He couldn't know who she was, but he was sharp enough to see that the carpeting looked just like the carpeting in my place, and he could guess.

"I wondered why her dog didn't bark," I said faintly, like it was at all relevant.

"They found the dog too," Sid said, his voice not really cut out for gentle. "The granddaughter and her boyfriend discovered them early this morning when they went over to take the old lady to breakfast. Found the dog's neck snapped and the old lady bled out. Coroner puts time of death at last night, around the same time your place was invaded."

I wanted to look away, but it seemed like some sort of self-punishment to make myself look. "It's all my fault," I said, finally glancing away before anyone could see my blood tears. "They wanted to get to *me*. They probably only attacked her to shut the dog up."

God, I didn't even know her name. We'd smiled at each other and exchanged a few words, the couple of times I'd been out to the apartment. Her dog had growled at me and she'd shushed him, even bringing me a plate of homemade cookies on moving day as an apology. She'd had such a sweet smile, just like the kind of grandma they put on TV commercials selling ice cream and apple pie.

I wiped away the tears and realized that my fangs had extended; I hoped it was in reaction to my own blood (though that was icky enough) and not to what I saw on the screen. I was very careful to talk around them, not so much for fear of slicing myself but to keep from lisping.

"Dion is dead meat." I'd think about the whole 'bringing him in alive' thing later. Much. "Brent and Marcy mentioned a last-known?"

"The police have been over it. Dion—Nelson Ricci—and his uncle have both cleared out."

"You're sure the uncle's gone and not... dead?"

"We don't know anything until we find him or his body."

"What about the ID checker at the club—you know, bleached blond, cat's-eye contacts?"

"No sign of her. She's not at her apartment or answering her phone."

"Crap."

"It sounds so cultured when you say it," Sid said dryly.

"Bite me," I answered.

He actually cracked a half-smile at the irony.

Then it hit me—a potential lead, someone I could pump for information, someone who wanted to be my new bestest friend. Well, I already had a bestie, but I was still in the market for an entourage. Sid's eyes widened when I slid two fingers into my cleavage to retrieve Hunter's card. *Charles Orloff, DDS,* it said. I wondered if he made his own faux fangs. I just couldn't quite picture it . . . I could see him as an ear, nose, and throat guy maybe, or a blood tech, whatever they called them, playing vampire on the weekends, but a mild-mannered *dentist*? With the paper bibs and their minty-flavored menace?

I flashed the card triumphantly. "Meet Hunter, vamp lifestyler and all-around adventurer with the Burgess Brigade, one of Tampa Bay's premier clans. Tell me, Sid, what do you know about human servants?"

• • •

The number on Hunter's card led to a voicemail with a second number for after-hours emergencies. I dialed the after-hours number and left a message, hoping Charles Orloff, DDS, didn't have a partner on call tonight.

"Hi, this is, ah—Cosette D'Ampir." He wouldn't know me by any other name. "It's an emergency that I speak with Dr. Orloff. Please have him call me back as soon as possible." I left my Fed cell phone number, then ended the call and looked at the others. "What now?"

Sid was unhooking his laptop from the other equipment in the room, preparing to pack it up. "I'm going to the new crime scene to liaise with the police. They're going to want into your apartment as well, and they're going to want to talk to you."

"So I should come with you?" I asked.

"No, you'll be tied up half the night if you do that. We told them about the vandalism to your place when we heard about your neighbor, and they're all pissy about the fact that we didn't let them know sooner, so I'm going to be doing a lot of political ass-kissing that you don't need to see. I'll give them your statement. No need for us all to waste our time, though I may have to turn you over for an interview at some point. You two get cleaned up. You smell like a smokehouse."

Bobby and I exchanged a *look*.

"*Separately!*" he barked. "Then check out Nelson Ricci's last-known address. The police have already been over it, but maybe you'll find something new, like a clue about where his uncle disappeared to and how to get in touch with him. Then you're on the other names Brent and Marcy dug up. I've cc'd you on the info." Sure enough, my phone vibrated to let me know I had new texts. "Marcy and Brent are still working the human-vampire scene. I don't want to blow their cover having them out interviewing families."

So Marcy got to play dress-up, and I got stuck playing Feeb. The kicker—it didn't even come with the hot Men-in-Black-style shades. Not that I'd ever been okay with standard issue, but in that case I might make an exception.

"Blood?" I asked.

"In the kitchenette. If you heat it up, wash the pots. That stuff tends to ... congeal."

I made a face at him, but he wasn't paying me any attention. At least, not until his laptop was all packed away in its carrying case. "Well, what are you waiting for?" he asked. "Go. I'll lock up on my way out."

See, *suspicious*. First this weird case, then all their uber-secrecy, which seemed excessive, even for spies. Weren't we all supposed to be on the same team?

"Why?" I asked. "In case we're tempted to make off with your big-screen TV?"

He glared. "This is sensitive equipment. It's not meant for video games or reruns of *The Bachelor*."

"*As if*," I said, at the same time Bobby burst out with, "You have video games?"

"No," Sid answered. "No games, no cable. Out."

Bobby and I exchanged another look, a whole lot less smoldering than the last.

We proceeded Sid out of the conference room and, sure enough, he locked it behind him.

"Don't dawdle," he ordered. "And check in when you get to the last-known."

I was tempted to salute, but he'd probably appreciate it, so I let it go.

"Dibs on the shower," I said, but only as cover until Sid was well and truly gone—out the door and into the night.

"Well, that was weird," Bobby said, heading for the room with the cots, probably to try and scrounge clean clothing.

"Wait." I put a hand on his arm to stop him. "This is the perfect chance to investigate—while we have the place to ourselves."

"You think they don't have surveillance here?"

"Hello, we've come face-to-face with the Mad Monk, fought off a psycho-psychic, and put the screws to the entire vampire council. You're afraid of a little surveillance? We don't even show up on camera, remember."

"I remember. Don't *you* remember about motion detectors, microphones, pressure switches—"

Now that he mentioned it… "Oh, right. Well, if they've got the place miked, we're already sunk."

"Look, I understand that you're concerned, but we've got to be smart about this. If there's something wrong, we've got to be inside the system to change it. We can't do that if we're locked up."

"Fine," I said testily, "*you* think. It's what you're good at. *I'll* act."

I was down the hallway before he could come up with an answer to that. But, as I knew he would, Bobby caught up to me. He just needed proper prodding.

I used the very bottom of my skirt to turn knobs and keep from leaving fingerprints. It had the side effect of revealing a fairly indecent amount of leg. Bobby, silently working the other side of the hallway, was flatteringly distracted. I even thought for a second that he was going to ditch the plan in order to check out my lack of visible panty lines when a door opened to him. There hadn't been many doors so far—the building was long, but not terribly wide—but it was a surprise, since all the others so far had been locked.

"Bathroom," he reported.

We didn't find a basement, but there were stairs leading up to a second floor, which we wasted no time exploring. The only open rooms there were the kitchenette Sid had mentioned and a full bath. It looked like the second story had been set up as a small apartment, in case the owner of the pawnshop wanted to live above it.

"I can start picking locks," I offered. I'd been really good at that in spy school, which stood to reason. I could do amazing things with eyeliner and an eyebrow pencil. Lock picking was just a different kind of precision work.

"Or I could tumble the locks with my mind," Bobby countered.

"Show-off."

"Just want to impress my girl."

My heart got all gooshy when he said things like that, which was just stupid. I was my own girl, thank you very much.

"Okay then, wow me." I crossed my arms beneath my cleavage to impress him right back.

Bobby's eyes flared. "You know," he said, "I'd much rather be searching you than this place."

My whole body heated up. I could picture him pushing me up against the hallway wall, kissing me to within an inch of my unlife, and finally sinking his fabulous fangs into my neck as I held him close. I pictured me trailing fingernails down his back, wrapping a leg around him ... Either Bobby was picking up on my thoughts or his fangs were totally on my wavelength already. They slid down into place as I watched. It would be so easy to turn fantasy into reality.

I couldn't believe *I* was going to be the voice of reason. "Sid's going to be waiting for our call. We'd better get a move on."

"When this is all over—" he promised. He didn't say anything more, but the images that filled my head were, well, *beyond.* My resolve wavered and I took a step forward, but Bobby'd turned back to the door, resisting temptation. Damn him. Oh right, too late.

Here's the kicker—it was all for nothing. The whole place, top to bottom, was completely sanitized, a shell, an empty place where secrets might visit but weren't allowed to live. We learned that Maya wore bikini briefs and that Sid was all about the tighty whities, which I could have told you without even looking. Beyond that—nothing. The Feds apparently ran a paperless office, and they'd taken their laptops with them. We didn't find so much as a disk or a thumb drive.

"Craptastic," I said, finally admitting to failure.

"Maybe there's nothing to find," Bobby soothed.

"Maybe not here, but somewhere."

He took me in his arms and kissed the top of my head, which he could do since even in my spiky heels I barely made it to five foot three, and he was almost six feet tall. It felt good. Too good. If I wasn't careful, I'd come to really crave him, and if there was one rule I lived by—beyond *moisturize* and *never let them see you sweat*—it was that the balance of power had to be maintained. Mine, that was. But I was starting to forget why losing myself in someone else was such a bad idea. My mother had taught me that counting on anyone else, even my own parents, was madness. That way lay dependency and vulnerability and other SAT words, but *this was Bobby.* He'd never been anything but good to me. Maybe in a decade or century or so he'd start taking me for granted. When the time came, I'd hit him upside the head with a clue-by-four. But for now … I melted into him and let him hold me. I even held him back. Fiercely.

"You're not going to let this go, are you?" he asked finally.

I pushed away reluctantly to look into those wicked blue eyes. "Would you?"

"Not if I thought I was right."

"Exactly."

He kissed me on the tip of my nose and then met it with his own. "How about that shower? Maybe we should disobey orders. Taking it together would save time and other resources."

Wow, Bobby offering to disobey orders. I met his smoldering gaze, then gave him a once-over from his fully erect canines to his fully erect ... libido ... and back up with a seductive grin.

"Somehow, I don't think that's going to save any time."

His answering smile could have started a five-alarm fire in a flood zone. "I think you're right."

7

In the interest of time, we reluctantly decided on separate showers after all.

When I got out of mine, my phone was vibrating on the cotside table, indicating a message that turned out to be from Dr. Charles Orloff, DDS. The message said that he had dinner plans, but he really wanted to meet around ten p.m. at some kind of wine bar on Vine.

I called back to make it a date, and almost forgot what I was going to say when a nearly naked Bobby entered the room, all glistening from his own shower with nothing but a tiny white towel around his waist that he had to hold closed with one hand. I'd, ah, sort of used the big ones on the rack for my body and hair and not returned them. They were, in fact, still in use.

"Want one of mine?" I asked, as I waited through the dental doc's voicemail greeting to leave my message.

Bobby, smiling in sweet seduction, took a step forward. My mouth went dry, the message beeped, and Bobby helped himself to the towel I was using as a turban, spilling my dark hair all over my face and shoulders.

I blew the hair out of my face and glared at Bobby as I struggled for words. "Hey, *Hunter*," I said in my sexiest voice. "It's a date. See you there."

I hung up and brushed the hair out of my face to glare more effectively, but Bobby didn't notice. He was too busy using the stolen towel to dry his dripping hair. I lunged for it and snapped it away. He lost his waist towel trying to grab it back with one hand while hiding himself with the other. I laughed at the sight, but the laughter quickly changed to appreciation of the view. I held the big towel up and away, hoping he'd come in for it, totally unprepared for his fake-out and grab for *my* body towel. I'd have caught it if my free hand hadn't still been holding my cell phone.

Suddenly the tables had turned. I was totally buck naked. I squeaked and reached for the sheets on the nearest cot, gripping them to me like I was some girly-girl heroine. Bobby laughed. "Got you!"

"I got you first!"

My phone played out the first few notes of the Su Surrus song *Bite Me*. "Damn," I said. With that ring tone, it was either Sid or Maya. Could they know what we'd been up to? Had we tripped some silent alarm? Crap!

I answered before it could go to voicemail. "Hey," I said, trying to sound breezy and innocent.

"You *do* know your phone has a GPS, right?" Sid asked without preamble.

"Um, I guess. I've never really thought about—"

"So I *know* you haven't left yet," he cut in. "Don't make me separate you two."

If I'd had any air in my lungs, I'd have sighed in relief. He thought we'd been fooling around. I mean, more than we actually were. He didn't know what we'd really been up to.

"We're leaving now." I gave Bobby a significant look, he gave me a raised brow—so cool, that—and I knew he was picking up on everything with his super-vamp hearing.

"You'd better be." Sid hung up again without even a good-bye.

"How quickly can you be ready?" Bobby asked.

I grabbed pre-stocked clothes out of the closet, scrunched my nose at the button-down mom-blouse and black slacks, and started to dress. "Five minutes, as long as you drive."

"What does that have to do—oh." Smart boy, my Bobby.

I'd seen an emergency supply of makeup in the bathroom. In a moving car, with no reflection, it would be tough to apply, but I'd manage. Failure was not an option. I wouldn't have time to blow-dry my hair, but as long as I could brush, flip, mousse, and scrunch, I'd be fine.

Bobby followed me toward the bathroom to keep me on track, but he didn't have to worry. I scooped up my supplies and turned. "Ready."

"Really?" he asked. He got over the surprise quickly and slipped an arm around my waist to steer me out the door before I could change my mind. Like I wouldn't know what he was up to.

Dion's place ... or at least, his place before he'd gone to ground ... had an air of neglect about it. Like no maid or maintenance guy had ever brushed away the cobwebs that seemed like a topcoat to the house's formerly white trim. The rest of the house was gray, occasionally patched with mis-matched, putty-toned stucco. The gardens had been turned over to the weeds, and the lawn was more thistle and clover than grass.

Bobby used his mojo to tumble the locks. He called it telekinesis, but mojo sounded way more Austin Powers, and since we were international vampires of mystery ...

Even knowing that the place was supposedly empty, that Dion's uncle was AWOL and Dion in the wind, Bobby called a "hello" into the house as we entered. Ever polite was my guy. When no one answered, he closed the door behind us.

But the place wasn't *completely* deserted. Something skittered across the floor in front of us. I shrieked and turned back for the door.

"Relax," Bobby said, grabbing my sleeve. "It was just a spider."

"Just? *Just?*" I answered, my voice rising. "It was the size of my *thumb.*"

"Okay, look, plug your ears."

"Why?"

"Trust me."

I plugged, feeling totally stupid standing in the middle of a spider sanctuary with my only weapons in my ears.

Bobby yelled at the top of his lungs, jumped up and down a few times, and generally behaved like he'd lost his mind.

I stared. When he didn't seem ready to erupt again, I lowered my hands. "What was *that* all about?"

"That was me announcing that we were the biggest, baddest dudes in the place and that anything with more than two legs ought to run for the hills."

"What hills? This is *Florida*."

"The figurative hills. Anyway, anything with a self-preservation instinct won't dare to scare, okay? We're all safe and sound."

I looked around, making sure not a creature was stirring. "Oo-kay, but if anything attacks, I'm counting on you to kill it. I don't do insects."

"Technically, a spider is an arachnid—"

"Bobby," I snapped.

"Right, you don't care. If it moves, I kill it. Happy?"

"Ecstatic."

"Good."

"Great."

"Fine."

"*Fine*," I finished, because everyone knew *fine* was the last word, and I wouldn't let him have it.

Anyway, we were standing in an entryway covered in bookshelves. They were everywhere we looked, lining every wall, bookending both sides of the television. The house had an open floor plan, so from where we stood we could see straight through the curtainless sliding glass doors to the enclosed sun porch. I half expected to see books stacked sky-high on the patio ... lanai ... whatever they called it here, as well. Instead ... well, I had no idea what I was looking at, really. There were work tables set up on pairs of sawhorses all throughout the room, with machines set out on them that would have sent the Burgess Brigade into flights of euphoria. They looked like high-tech steampunk engines with exposed wires, gears, gages, and flaps. Around them, a machine shop had exploded. Parts and tools were everywhere. Covering some of them were books that had wandered away from the shelves, set wide open and face down, pages being mashed. Bobby gasped and moved toward the gadgets, eyes reverent, like a kid coming into a double-decker candy shop.

"You take the patio," I said generously, since he'd have a way better idea than me of what we were looking at. "I'll, uh, find Dion's room."

Bobby nodded distractedly, already mesmerized.

Off the living room were two alcoves that led to short hallways. I picked the closest. There were three rooms off of it. The bathroom in the center had "bachelor pad" written all over it: standard white walls, no decoration, matte-black shower curtain, faded black towels, stubble in the sink, and shaving cream, razor, aftershave, deodorant, toothbrush, and crusted-up toothpaste tube scattered about the counter. The toilet seat was up, of course. The overriding smell was sweat and aftershave. In short, it was just like thousands of other bathrooms without a woman's touch or any chance of inviting one.

I closed the door quickly, before the shaggy shavings could rise up against me. To the left was a room Dion and his uncle apparently used as an office. There were filing cabinets lining one wall with papers sticking out every which way and more stacked on top. Another wall held a desk with more paper-work, a computer, webcams, speakers, and two printers ... or maybe one was a scanner. Anyway, more gadgetry than I could decipher. Since paperwork didn't require a password, I started with the low-tech, sitting at the desk in order to sort. The stack to the right was gobbledygook. At a guess, Dion's uncle was some kind of work-from-home computer consultant. The correspondence was all geek to me.

The stack to the left seemed to be personal—nothing very interesting until I came to the flyers for inventors' shows, parts and component swaps, denials of patents and angry, half-written letters of protest. I didn't understand all the technical stuff that was rattled off, but Dion's uncle—Eric Ricci—quickly devolved from scientist to nutbar as his letters went on. The gist from the Patent Office seemed to be that his devices didn't work, and his responses boiled down to "Do too," and accusations of crazy government conspiracies publicly denying and privately stealing his plans.

"Hey, Bobby!" I yelled. "You've got to see this!"

He was at the other end of the house, but vamp senses had their perks. He was with me in seconds.

"It's crazy," he said from the doorway, as if reading my mind. "He's got notebooks filled with specs and data, dozens of machines, but none of them seem to function."

Wow, were we on the same wavelength or what?

"They don't. Look, notes from the Patent Office, paranoid rants back. Dion's uncle was totally delusional." I held up some of the massive paperwork.

"Find anything about a second home? A studio? A storage space even?"

"Not yet, but look at all this crap. It'd take a year and a team of forensic … uh, paper-ologists to go through it."

"Paper-ologists, huh?"

"Whatever."

"Well, they've got us, so we'd better get to it."

I rolled my eyes.

"I'll take the cabinets," he offered.

An hour later, he'd moved over to the computer, but his mental mojo didn't work on encryption, just physical barriers, and we struck out. I was starting to go a little nuts myself.

"Why don't you finish up here, and I'll move on to Dion's room," I said finally, because right now, even eau de teenaged boy seemed preferable to paperwork.

"Uh huh," he answered, distracted, as if he'd actually found something interesting in the wreckage.

I escaped before he could pull me back in. The last door off the hallway was Dion's, if the lack of machinery was any indication. He had a loft bed and the usual sorts of furniture—dresser, armoire open to expose a television and gaming system—but it was impossible to get to any of it without wading through pants, socks, T-shirts, dishes, and things I seriously didn't want to identify but that reeked of athletic supporter. It looked like someone had hit the eject button on his laundry hamper. In all, the house wasn't quite *Hoarders*-level insanity, but *Clean Sweep* would probably have a field day.

"Uh, trade you," I called out to Bobby.

He appeared in the doorway, took one look around, and let a wolfish grin spread across his face. "Bet I'm looking pretty good right about now."

"You'll look even better if you take over. Seriously, anything could be living under here," I said, indicating the top layer of filth.

"Not if it needs to breathe." His nose crinkled in a totally endearing way. He was just too ridiculously cute, really. "Come on, we'll tackle it together."

It might have been the first time in my life I was completely uninterested in being in a bedroom with Bobby. If there was a little black book, the police had already found it. There were no real estate listings with tell-tale Sharpie circles, no Google maps or mysterious phone numbers on napkins, no mad manifesto…it was a wash, and I said so.

"Well, crud," Bobby said, "crap" being apparently a little too edgy for him, and "shit" not even an option. "I do *not* want to check in with Sid empty-handed. Where to next?"

"Do you have the address of the vanishing vampiress from the club?"

"Yeah."

"Then let's hit it. Call it women's intuition."

"You have that?"

I gave him a glare. *"Hello*, I'm a woman. It's like our own special superpower."

He didn't look convinced, but he was a guy. What did he know?

The vanishing meet-and-greet girl from the Tower—or Bleached Blond Vampiress (BBV), as I'd chosen to call her—turned out not to live in Tampa but in a nearby town called Lutz, which I wanted to pronounce like the ice skating move, lutz, as in klutz without the k. Bobby said it was supposed to rhyme with "shoots," which made me wonder why they didn't just spell it that way then. While we were at it, I told him, the whole English language could totally use a make-over. In tough economic times, didn't it make total sense to drop the silent "k" from knife, and the "p" from things like psychology? Just think of all the paper that could be saved. I mean, books would be, like, a third shorter. Complete financial sense, right?

Bobby looked at me like I'd lost it and started arguing about all the money that would be blown updating dictionaries, thesauruses, spell-checkers, etc., but I thought he was just being a killjoy. I could revolutionize the English language.

Anyway, it turned out that BBV, Elise Radner, lived in a small white house with turquoise trim centered on a side street off the oddly named Dale Mabry Highway. If Dale Mabry was someone special, he was so obscure that even my brainy boy had no idea who he was. We cruised past the house, just surveying it this pass. No lights. No movement, except for the swaying palm tree in the front yard. A goth living in a perky place with palm trees ... it was just weird. Bobby parked on an offshoot of the side street, car turned so that we could make a quick getaway if need be.

The cops needed probable cause and a warrant to enter the place, but we were totally covert ops. We didn't have to worry about things like that. Bobby and I pulled blue latex gloves out of a box in the glove compartment and pocketed them for when we got inside. Luckily, with Bobby's mental mojo, we shouldn't even have to touch the outside. The gloves would have been totally too conspicuous to wear strolling through the neighborhood, even if they did match Bobby's eyes and add a nice splash of color to my black-and-white outfit.

We tried knocking first—on a turquoise door that matched the trim. It would have seemed almost absurdly cheerful except that the door knocker was a little brass gargoyle clutching the ring in its talons and the door mat on which we stood announced, *Solicitors will be eaten. Everyone else, welcome!*

"Meddle not in the affairs of dragons," Bobby muttered, "for you are crunchy and good with ketchup."

"What?" I asked, giving him back the look he'd given me in the car.

"Ah, nothing. Something I read once on a T-shirt. The mat reminded me of it."

"Uh huh."

Not surprisingly, no one came to the door to let us in. My vamp hearing couldn't pick up a thing from inside, so BBV wasn't making a run for it out the back door. The place felt dead.

"Door," I said to Bobby.

He obliged, using his mojo to tumble the locks and turn the knob. He pretended, for anyone on the quiet street who might notice, to be greeting someone inside, pushed the door open with his knuckles, and walked in. I followed, bumping the door shut behind me with a hip.

It wasn't a very big house, but the entry led right into an airy floor plan. The high ceilings made it seem airy, anyway. A small dining room area was separated from the living room only by the placement of the couch—lime green with, what else, turquoise pillows. I scrunched my nose. The kitchen was visible from the rest of the house via a half-wall that doubled as a breakfast bar. Or, it would have been visible if not for the towering stacks of mail that blocked the view. The stacks didn't look disturbed; the bar stools still stood upright; dishes were in the sink, dirty but all in one piece. The place was intact. No signs of struggle. Not that I'd expected any.

Bobby and I pulled on our gloves.

"You want to take the bedrooms?" I asked him. I'd already had enough of tighty whities to last an entire night, although I suspected BBV was a thong kind of girl.

"Okay. Let me know if you find anything interesting."

He disappeared into the hallway off the living room, and I started on the mail. Bill, bill, catalogue, catalogue, latest issues of *Modern Goth, Fangoria,* and *Rue Morgue,* sales flyers. Not a personal letter in the bunch, though I did notice a few envelopes addressed to Kinesha Williams rather than Elise Radner.

"Hey, Bobby," I called out. "Any Kinesha Williams connected with the case?"

He popped his head back into the hallway. "When I was working with Sid and Maya on the background checks, we looked up recent missing persons reports, especially for young people who'd gone missing within the last couple of weeks. Her name was on the list."

"I don't suppose it was her roommate who reported her missing?"

"Elise?" Bobby asked.

"Yup."

"No, it was her parents."

"Elise was never questioned?"

"I don't think she came up. Kinesha had just moved out on her own, according to them. They didn't like her living alone. That's why they panicked right away when they didn't hear from her for a couple of days."

"I don't think she got far," I said sadly. I hoped she wasn't another victim of the killer kids.

It didn't surprise me that Bobby remembered all that from

the missing person report. He had the kind of mind where if you just flipped through the phone book in front of him, he could probably reel off the phone number for the third, fourth, or tenth John Smith down the page without breaking a sweat. I was lucky I remembered my car keys.

With a frowny face, Bobby went back to what he'd been doing and I continued on into BBV's kitchen. The smell from the sink was nearly overwhelming. I'm not sure it would have been to purely human senses, but to mine— ugh. Congealed meatloaf, garlic mashed potatoes ... my eyes watered blood. I nearly gagged and retreated, but something caught my bleary eyes on the small chef's rack that seemed to double as a bookcase.

I brushed away my bloody tears and squatted beside the books on the lower part of the rack. I ran my gloves over the spines. They stayed starkly blue, which meant that either Elise was a helluva housekeeper, which contradicted the evidence in the sink, or the books hadn't just been sitting around collecting dust. I wasn't interested in the cookbooks, but the others—*The Black Veil, The Madness of Mobs, Sanguine Seduction, Bacchanals,* and ... *The Cult of Dionysus.*

I wondered ... could Dion be short for Dionysus? Had I maybe found a connection?

Footsteps approached. I grabbed the book off the shelf and turned to show Bobby, just as my world exploded. Agony flashed like a firebomb across my temple. My vision went purple with pain, and I fell to the ground. The book skidded away from me. I kicked out frantically, trying to catch my attacker in the shin, crotch, whatever I could reach.

"Cosette?" my attacker gasped.

Then I heard another blow fall and he *oophed.*

Bobby! I thought, trying to blink away the lava-lamp amoebas of purple pain so I could help.

I only got flashes of visibility—Bobby and ... *Ballard?* Yes, Ballard, with a gnarled wood cane flailing around ineffectively in an attempt to whack Bobby on the head and dislodge him. But Bobby had him in some kind of super hold we'd learned in training. Plus, human vs. vamp ... Ballard had no chance.

I caught the cane as it flailed my way and yanked it from Ballard before he hurt anyone else. No wonder I'd gone down. Wood was like vampire kryptonite. Oh, Bobby had a lot to answer for when I started thinking in *Superman* references. Or maybe I was still woozy from the blow to the head.

"Everybody calm down," I ordered.

I used the cane to stabilize myself as I rose to my feet again. Wood was okay as long as it wasn't breaking the skin. Speaking of which—I put my free hand to my head and it came away wet with blood. Which explained why my fangs were out in full force.

Ballard looked wild-eyed. "Cosette? What are you doing here? What—?" He caught sight of the fangs and went as stiff as a board. "Those aren't clip-ons, are they?"

Wow, I was totally hot at this covert stuff.

"I think the question is, what are *you* doing here," Bobby asked, squeezing him for information ... literally.

Ballard wheezed and Bobby lightened up just a bit. "Chill, chill!" Ballard croaked. "I was just checking on Elise. She never came to work today, never called in. She's not answering her phone. When I showed up here the door was unlocked, so I let myself in and found you. I thought Cosette was an intruder."

"We never heard a phone ring," Bobby protested, tightening his grip again.

"Her cell phone," Ballard choked. "She doesn't have a landline."

"You're in the habit of bashing people over the head first and asking questions later?" I asked, not at all ready to let him off the hook.

He winced. "These murders have me on edge. I mean, first Dion goes off the deep end, then Elise disappears ... For all I knew you were part of Dion's crew and Elise was lying dead somewhere. She isn't, is she?" he asked, eyes nearly bugging out at the thought.

I relaxed a little. I was no truth-teller, but he was either sincere or a wicked-good actor. I didn't think it was the latter.

"Why don't you let him go and we'll sit down and talk about it? Ballard won't try anything, will you Ballard?"

"No, *he won't*," Bobby answered for him. I knew he was putting some of his special emphasis behind it, because I could feel his power wash over Ballard, charging the air like an electrical storm.

Ballard nodded his head in dazed agreement and Bobby let him go, guiding him over to Elise's small dining room table and chairs. We all sat.

"So, you and Elise work together?" I asked.

Ballard looked at me, focusing in on my fangs, which still hadn't retracted. I was used to pervy guys staring, but not at my mouth—not unless I was licking my lips or oh-so-casually applying gloss. I closed my lips over the fangs as best I could, trying not to think of blood so they'd retract. It was like trying not to think of shopping while at a mall. Not even *in*humanly possible.

"At the movie theater," Ballard said. "Actually, she's my manager. It's really out of character for her to ditch. Can I feel them?" he asked.

I drew back, shocked, before I remembered we were talking about my teeth.

"Maybe," I said, feeling really weird about it, "if you tell us what we want to know."

Bobby gave me a look, like my fangs should totally be off-limits to other guys. I gave him a "get real" glance back.

"Like what?" he asked.

"Okay, she's your manager," Bobby said. "How do you know where she lives?"

"We hang." He looked back to me as he said, "Sometimes we hook up."

"When was the last time you saw her?" Bobby asked.

"*That* way or, you know, socially?"

"Either one."

"Last night at the club. Cosette—or whoever you are—you met her."

I nodded.

"But then you disappeared," he continued. "And she disappeared. Tonight you turn up here."

He said it like a question I wasn't going to answer.

"I'm here and she isn't," I said instead. "Moving right along—do you know of anywhere else she might be? If she wanted to get away for a while, where would she go?"

"I don't know. She's been kind of strange lately. Like, restless. She was starting to wonder whether Dion and the others had the right idea—striking out on their own, starting their own society. The vampire court wasn't getting her any closer to where she wanted to be. But that was before the murders," he added quickly. "She's not a freak or anything like that. I mean, she wouldn't . . . " But he trailed off as if he wasn't really so sure.

"Where did Dion and Elise want to be?" Bobby asked.

"Immortal. Forever young. All of that. Most of us in the *lifestyle* . . . well, we know that's what it is, a lifestyle, a philosophy, a way of being. But *they* were convinced it could be more. Now?" he asked, and I realized we were still talking about my fangs.

"Not yet," I answered. "Did they ever ask you to join them? Do you know where they meet?"

"Elise sounded me out, but there was just something about Dion that didn't seem right. He'd changed, and not for the better. I don't know where they meet. You think they got Elise, don't you?"

"Define *got*," Bobby said.

"Shit."

"If she isn't with them, where would she go?" I asked.

"You mean, if she were afraid or something? I don't know. Maybe her mom's. We hooked up there a few times, back when Elise had a roommate."

"Kinesha Williams?" I asked.

He looked at me, fascination starting to turn to fear. "Who *are* you people?"

I just smiled, letting my fangs do all the talking. Fear was fun.

"Yeah, Kinesha," he said, swallowing hard. "She moved out last week. Said things were getting too weird."

"Go figure. We're going to need Elise's mom's address," I told him.

"Okay, but they're not close."

He called the address up on his phone and recited it to us. "And yours," I insisted. The look he gave me indicated he thought maybe I had ulterior motives, like a hook-up of my own. As if. I mean, he was hot enough, but compared to my boy, Bobby…Besides, he'd just hit me over the head with a cane. Not exactly my idea of foreplay.

"Now can I touch?"

"Knock yourself out." I pulled my lips back from my teeth to give him access to my fangs and shivered as he touched them. It wasn't so much the touch that affected me, but the closeness of all that blood just beneath his skin. With his fingers resting on my lips, I could feel his pulse, smell his scent—spicy, like he'd had Indian food earlier in the day. Yes, I'd helped myself to that bottled blood back at headquarters, but it was nothing next to the fresh stuff straight from the vein. With a will of its own, my tongue crept forward to taste his flesh. Ballard closed his eyes, breathing hard.

"*Hello*, remember me?" Bobby cut in.

"We can share," I offered.

Ballard drew back, the spell broken. "What?"

"Nothing. Thank you for your help. We'll be in touch."

His hand dropped to his side. "Hunter does nice work," he said. "Maybe I'll have him do mine."

I almost laughed—here I'd thought I was giving my true nature away. I looked at Bobby to see whether he'd planted the suggestion in Ballard's mind that my fangs were permanent dental implants, but he shook his head slightly. Apparently

Ballard, for all he was nicknamed after a writer, couldn't even *imagine* the reality of us. One less loose end to worry about.

Bobby was busily texting the new names and addresses to Sid.

"Come on," I said to Ballard. "I'll walk you out."

He looked disappointed. "What about Elise?"

"Call us if you hear from her. Or see her. *Do not* let her into your place or meet up with her in any dark alleys, okay?"

"You think she's one of them now? Dion's crew?" he asked.

"I think you're better safe than sorry." I gave Ballard my number and closed the door on his shell-shocked look.

"Sid wants us to check on Elise's mother."

"*Check on*, not 'interview'?" I asked. Bobby was usually so precise.

"Well, given what happened to Kelly Swinter's family when she apparently joined up—"

"You think it's some kind of initiation?"

"Not enough of a sample to draw a conclusion."

"Ah, geek speak. I'm not asking you to stake your reputation on it. I'm just asking what you *think*."

"It's possible."

I checked the readout on my phone. There was plenty of time before my appointment with Hunter. "Okay then, I'll drive."

"But—"

"You'll do that Goody Two-shoes obeying-the-speed-limit thing."

"It's safer—"

"Someone's life might hang in the balance," I said, with my usual flare for the dramatic.

"I'd say definitely, the way you drive—"

I blew him a raspberry, shoved Elise's Dionysus book into his hands to keep them busy, and frisked him for the car keys. Predictably, the distraction worked. Bobby was totally mesmerized by the book, flipping pages as he followed me out to the car. Now, if I tried to walk and read at the same time, I'd probably break my neck, but I had the feeling it wasn't the first time for him. Unfortunately, it had the side effect of slowing him down just a bit, so that I had the car in gear before his door was even shut. I took off the second his foot cleared the pavement, the forward thrust slamming the door shut for him.

Bobby nearly toppled into my lap and came up cursing— or as close as he ever came to it. "Darn it, Gina, a second more or less—"

"Might mean everything to Mrs. R," I finished for him.

"So might solving this whole mystery. How much of this book did you read?"

"I, uh, skimmed. It's all about a cult, right? Sounds totally relevant."

"Yeah, you did good. Dionysus was the Greek god of wine, fertility, and basically lack of inhibitions. His rituals were … bloody doesn't even begin to cover it. He had female followers called the Bacchae who would go into religious frenzies, ripping people apart with their bare hands. All part of the fertility thing. You know, life from death. A lot of religions have it. Native Americans have Corn Woman; Ancient Egyptians have Osiris's dismembered body fertilizing Isis and giving birth to Horus. Christianity has Jesus and Lazarus both rising from the dead … "

"Fascinating," I said, "but what does all this have to do with us?"

"Think about it . . . what else rises from the dead?" he asked.

"Well, duh, *vampires*, but—" I had the sudden urge to bang my head against the steering wheel. "*Of course!* Vampires feed on blood. They rise from the dead. Do you think Dion's got his cult convinced that from death comes life?"

"It's a theory."

Which meant "Yes."

8

Fire trucks and police cars flew past us as we approached the Radner place, and I started to get a very bad feeling about what we'd find when we got there. Bobby white-knuckled the dashboard, but didn't complain as I slipped in close behind an ambulance and let it clear our path.

"Damn, damn, damn," Bobby chanted under his breath; the language was so unusual for him, it nearly shocked me into an accident. "Dead ends everywhere."

"Let's hope not."

"Slow down!" Bobby yelled suddenly.

I slammed on the brakes in reaction, even though I wasn't about to hit that hydrant. Really. I swear.

"That's Kelly Swinter's car," he said in explanation, pointing at a little blue hatchback.

"How do you know?"

Bobby looked at me in disbelief. "I read the file."

"Oh, well … sure."

The police already had the street around the house blocked off and the firefighters were firing up their hoses. But we couldn't wait for the flames to be subdued. Not if Mrs. R might be burning up on the inside, along with any evidence needed to track down the firestarters.

I double-parked, blocking Kelly's car into its spot, and Bobby and I were out within milliseconds and racing toward the house. A police officer saw and tried to stop us, but we were too fast for him.

"My aunt!" I yelled as cover. Not that it mattered. We were getting into that house and there was nothing anyone could do about it.

Bobby kicked in the front door and the flames roared out at us, hungry for the inrushing oxygen, but he didn't even stop. He dashed right through and I followed behind him, the heat so bad I was instantly flush with blood sweat. It dripped into my eyes, and I wiped it away with my sleeve. My white shirt would never be the same again, but I didn't count that as much of a loss.

"Which way?" Bobby asked, when we were immediately faced with a staircase and several pathways off the foyer—one that led to a sunken living room, the rug already aflame, the kitchen beyond that, and a hallway off to the right.

"You go up, I'll go back," I ordered.

He nodded and ran, and I loved him for it. He respected my auth-or-it-TAY, as Cartman would say.

I dashed for the back of the house through the living room, which was empty of life. I hit the kitchen, thankful I didn't need to breathe. The smoke was thick like low-lying fog, but I pushed my way through it, and ... stopped dead in the kitchen entry. There was a body, but it was still breathing, and held upright by a teenaged guy. Dion, aka Nelson Ricci, in the flesh. All five feet eight inches of monobrow menace and Roman nose (roamin' all over his face, my mother would say). I sensed it would all work for him when he grew into it, but I wasn't inclined to give him that chance. Right now he was accessorizing with a barely breathing body. It wasn't doing anything for him.

Bobby, kitchen! I called mentally.

"I know that look," Dion said, voice gravelly beyond his years. From the smoke? "But he won't reach you in time, Gina."

I didn't know which to process first—the threat, the way he'd guessed about the mind-speak, or the fact that he knew my real name.

Then I heard the movement behind me. I ducked and whirled, one leg out to sweep anyone sneaking up on me straight off their feet. I almost didn't recognize the girl jumping my outswept leg like she was skipping rope. She came down hard, a manic gleam in her eye, clearly hoping to land all her weight on the leg, but I was already up and launching myself at her with my fingers together, hand bladed, aiming straight for the soft spot on her neck between the collar bones. One powerful blow there and she'd drop like a stone, with about as much breath. Big blue eyes widened above her button nose as she saw me coming and stumbled back.

Just as I made contact, something hard and heavy hit me in the back of the head. My blow still fell on the girl—Kelly Swinter—but it lost something in the execution as my skull cracked and pain shot through me.

I caught sight of my sneak attacker, Elise, just as my vision blacked, and another blow caught me as I was still reeling from the first. I fell to my hands and knees, but my pain sensors were already on overload and I didn't even feel myself hit the floor.

"We've got to get out of here *now*," Kelly choked out, her attempt at speech causing a coughing fit.

"Grab the girl," Dion ordered.

Behind me, something hit the ground hard, but I couldn't see who or what. My world narrowed to darkness and pain and threatened to wink out altogether. But I wasn't going down without a fight.

I lashed out a hand to grab … something … to pull myself upright. Whatever I caught cried out. Kelly? Elise? Definitely female. Flesh gave under my fingers, and whatever I held buckled under them. I collapsed back onto the floor with my failure, losing my grip.

"Gina!" someone called. The sound ricocheted through my head like a bullet, ripping through my brain, blowing apart what was left of my mind. Bobby. He'd come at my call. Must have been the cause of whatever had fallen beside me.

I blinked frantically to clear away the dark veil over my vision. I needed to see what was going on. To help Bobby and … someone. It was all so hard to *think*. Too many blows to the head. The scene wouldn't resolve itself into any more than a blur of shadows. I saw someone tall and broad-shouldered— had to be Bobby—and a blur of bleached blond hair sailing at him like a guided missile. When Bobby knocked her away with ease, Dion launched Mrs. R's unresisting body at him, only it fell on me instead of him, blotting out my world.

There was blood everywhere. I could smell it, even if I couldn't see. My teeth extended, and before I'd even formed a thought, I rolled, trying to throw off Mrs. R's body. I *wouldn't* drink from her, but all the others were fair game ... anyone I could reach. My hands became claws, scrabbling at the kitchen floor to propel me forward, toward the nearest blood-scent. Something flew past me and landed with an *oomph*, teeth clacking together—a sound I knew well from recent experience. I didn't hesitate or wait to see who I had. I struck blindly, my bloodlust leading the way. My teeth sank into flesh. A thigh? A calf? Either way, not hairy enough to be Dion's. It didn't matter. Blood flowed just the same, hot and tangy. Life itself. I lost myself in the release of blood flooding my mouth with a rush that was equal parts pain and euphoria—the pain as my body came back online, my bones reknit, and the bleeding into my brain reversed itself.

I'd have passed out or spontaneously combusted or just died from the overload of pleasure/pain to my system if I hadn't been tethered to life by, literally, the skin of my teeth. It was only when I realized that the flood had slowed to a sluggish stream that my fangs retracted. Horrified, I blinked my vision clear, but now the storm clouds of smoke inside the house were making that difficult. I could barely make out paling skin and scads of hair, beneath which I sought a pulse point. Someone grabbed me under the arms suddenly and hauled me away before I could find it.

"I've got you, Gina." It was Bobby. Thank God.

"But—"

"We've got to get *out*. The place is fully engulfed."

"But the body!" I said, my tongue barely cooperating.

"Mrs. Radner is out. I took care of her first." He sounded ashamed of that, like I should have been his first concern, even though I was a vampire and could handle everything better than poor Mrs. R. It was kind of sweet.

A zing of fear went through me at the thought. Had I killed? I remembered not being too concerned as I fed in my haze of hurt, but now…

"The others?" I asked.

I had a horrible feeling about all this. If I hadn't killed my victim, the fire would. I'd surely left her too weak to escape. I couldn't live with that, especially not for all eternity.

"There's no time!"

As if to punctuate his sentence, a beam or railing fell somewhere in the house with a great crack. Bobby pulled me toward the exit. Despite the fact that I was recovering, I didn't have the strength to resist.

"We've got to talk to the police," Bobby said.

"Turn myself in, you mean?"

Bobby turned so that he could look into my eyes. *"What?* Gina, anyone left in there is there because of the choices they made, not because of you."

"But—"

"But nothing. I saw. You fed. It's what we do. You

wouldn't have taken so much if they hadn't ambushed and hurt you, right?"

I nodded, not truly believing but lacking the will to argue.

"So it was self-defense. Someone was going down. It was either her or you."

It made sense; I just didn't buy it. I'd needed to feed, but *so much?*

"Look, I've got to get Mrs. Radner to the paramedics. We'll talk more later."

He hefted Mrs. R from the ground outside, where he'd laid her to go after me, and carried her cradled against his chest in a honeymoon hold. I didn't want to talk more. I wanted a do-over on the night. I followed after Bobby, barely remembering to cough and wheeze as if I'd inhaled all that thick smoke. The EMTs came forward right away, one shoving an oxygen mask over my face and another grabbing a gurney for Mrs. R and getting straight to work on her. I was relieved that the mask meant I didn't have to talk to anyone yet. I wasn't ready. The way I was feeling right now, I'd confess to murder. That wouldn't help anyone, and I had a personal score to settle with Dion. He was going down.

Bobby gave our statement. I saw him flash credentials, something I didn't have on me. Then he waved toward our car, probably describing the Swinter vehicle beside it. In another minute and he and his officer friend were coming toward me.

"Ma'am, I'm going to need your statement as well," the officer said when they reached me.

I cringed and removed my mask. The oxygen continued to hiss out, with the weird plastic smell it had picked up going through the tubing.

"Agent Crandall here says you got a tip that led to this house."

I licked my lips and prepared to lie through my teeth as *Agent Crandall* had done. "The tip said Mrs. Radner was in there, but it turned out to be an ambush. When we ran in, they were waiting for us. I can't tell you much more than that. I got clipped in the head and blacked out. When I came to, Agent Crandall was pulling me out of the burning house."

He nodded. "Have the paramedics checked you out?"

"I've got a very hard head."

He nodded again and I tried not to picture him as a bobblehead, but it was tough. I think my mind was desperately trying for some comic relief. "Anything you can remember would be a help."

I described Dion in all his monobrowed menace and as much as I could remember about Elise and Kelly. I'd seen the latter's picture during our initial briefing, but the psycho eyes she'd been sporting had turned her all but unrecognizable. They didn't really go with the button nose and bright blue eyes. Elise hadn't changed a bit, except for the absence of her cat's-eye contacts.

My cell phone interrupted the questioning, and I grabbed it out of my pocket to check the readout. *Hunter.* Crap, I'd forgotten all about him.

"I've got to take this," I told the officer. "Confidential informant."

He nodded like he understood and courteously turned away, but he didn't go far. He was talking to the EMTs about Mrs. R. The firefighters were still battling the blaze, but it didn't look like much of the house would be saved. Poor Mrs. R.

"Hello," I said, answering just before it kicked over to voicemail.

"Where are you? We said ten o'clock, right?"

I pulled the phone away from my ear to look at the time. Almost ten thirty. Crap again.

"Sorry! I ran into some ... trouble. Can you hang tight another half hour? Bar tab's on me."

He didn't answer for a second and I was afraid I was losing him, but finally he said, "Okay, but if you're not here by eleven, I'm gone."

I hung up and Officer Bobblehead met my eyes. "We have to go," I said. "My informant's not going to wait all night."

He ... wait for it ... nodded. "I know where to find you if I have any more questions." That was news to me, but I supposed Bobby must have given him a card or something.

I didn't want to go to a wine bar ... or anywhere but bed. It had been a busy night. I wasn't just tired, I was completely drained. This spy stuff sucked. Death sucked. Destruction sucked. And I sucked most of all. The girl I'd fed from—I wasn't going to think about it. I could beat myself up later, when I had time and privacy. For now, I had to pull myself together.

Luckily or unluckily, my very scent was a distraction. For the second night in a row, I was doomed to smell like a smokehouse. I wished I had the superpower of clean. "Got a brush and some wipes?" I asked Bobby, flashing back to the night I'd dug my way out of the grave.

"Glove compartment," he said with a smile.

I dug around and did the best I could with what I could find. I rolled my sleeves up to cover the blood I'd wiped from my forehead, unbuttoned an extra button on the blouse to distract from anything I missed and figured I was as ready as I was going to get.

"You going for an interview or a date?" Bobby asked.

"Date," I answered, poking at him. "Want to come along? I might need backup."

"The guy's a *dentist*," Bobby scoffed.

"Ever seen *Little Shop of Horrors*?"

He huffed. "I'm already your chauffeur. I might as well be your muscle too. Nothing I like better than watching you make eyes at some other guy."

"You know I only have eyes for you," I answered as he started up the car. It scared me because it was very nearly true.

I looked away from him so he'd break eye contact and focus on pulling out onto the road ... *and* because I didn't want him to know I was sincere. I had to keep him on his toes. Guys get comfy and all of the sudden they're taking you for granted, showing up empty-handed for dates—no flowers or candies or, better yet, sparklies, or missing dates altogether for brews and bromance with their buds ...

We hit the wine bar at 10:59, and I jumped out before the car even shut off to make sure I got to Hunter in time. He sat at a corner booth, back to the wall so he could watch the whole room, just like Bobby had the night before. On the table in front of him was a nearly empty bottle and a wine glass the size of a small fishbowl, with about an inch of something that looked like blood but probably wasn't. A hostess tried to seat me as I entered, but I waved her off and made a beeline for Hunter.

Behind me, I heard Bobby come in and chat with the hostess, who needed to see some ID before she'd seat him. Sometimes I forgot we were still supposed to be teens... *were* teens, except that I totally felt so much older than my old, pre-vamp self. Maybe it was even showing on my face, since the hostess hadn't carded me. Spy games, death, and destruction will do that to a girl. The double D's—death and destruction—made me think of the Radner place, and that made me think of... I immediately pushed it out of my head again. I could self-destruct later.

I pasted on a smile and stood beside Hunter's booth. "Is this seat taken?"

He'd been watching me since I entered, but it took him a beat to focus on my face, either because of the booze or because he'd seen something he liked below the neckline.

"No, please sit."

He was clearly expecting me to take the seat across from him, but I'd been jumped from behind once that night, and it was enough. I scooted him in and sat close enough to feel his heat. It was one thing I missed about being human—that warmth. Not that the cold really affected me anymore, but that roasty toasty feeling, like when you just wake up from a good sleep, all bundled under the covers... gone.

Hunter took a sip of his blood-red wine and swirled it around in his mouth for a second before swallowing.

"Look," he said when he wouldn't dribble, "I've already been through this conversation about six times on my own while I was waiting for you. What do you say we cut right to the chase?"

"Works for me." Especially given my level of exhaustion and my absolute commitment to getting the bastards responsible as soon as inhumanly possible.

"Good. What is it you want?" he asked.

"All the dirt you have on Dion, his associates, and the vampires behind the Tower."

His eyes widened. "But you're one of them."

"Yes and no."

He studied me, wary now. "What do I get in return?"

I studied him back. "What do you want?"

"Eternal life. I want you to bite me and do ... whatever it is you do so that I'll become one of you when I die."

I drew back from him despite his warmth. "Let's say that's even possible. Have you really thought about it? You won't be able to walk in the light. It'd kill your practice, because even if you cater to the night owls, you can't risk infecting your patients all unknowing if you nick yourself on something. How will you get by?"

"I'll worry about that later, after I'm dead. But I'll live a normal life until then, right? Knowing I'll rise again, I can plan—smart investments, a living will, that sort of thing. By the time I die, making a living won't be a problem."

"No, you'll have all-new problems, like sunlight and stakes."

"*You* did it," he said, eyes flashing.

"No, it was done *to* me." And look where I was now. Federal flunky—kicking butts and leaving them to burn in a fiery inferno. No, no, no, I didn't know that for sure. Maybe she'd gotten out. Maybe—

His eyes lost some of their burn. "I'm sorry you got turned against your will."

I shrugged, letting him buy that explanation for my pain. "Not your fault. But why ask me? Why not go to the devils you know?"

He looked away. "They won't do it. They won't even hear me out. Rules, they say. Maybe after a lifetime of service..."

"Seems a small price to pay for eternity."

"But, like you say, I have a life."

"So you want to have your cake and eat it too. Why didn't you join Dion's group, then? Aren't they promising a path to eternity?" That was totally the theory, anyway, given the cult of Dionysus and that whole life-from-death discussion.

"You know what they say—the road to hell is paved with large intestines." He stopped at the look on my face. "Sorry, bad joke. What I'm trying to say is that their path seems to involve a blood war."

"Go on."

He sat back in the booth and crossed his arms. "You haven't made me any promises yet. I'm not saying another word until we have a deal."

Stupid smart people.

"You *do* realize I could just mesmerize you, right? Force you to tell me what I want to know." I wasn't so sure my mojo was up to it, actually, but he didn't have to know that.

Hunter looked smug. "That's why we're meeting in a bar."

"Huh?"

"Too hard to mesmerize someone under the influence."

"Where did you come up with that?"

"P. N. Elrod—*The Vampire Files.*"

"What vampire files?"

"*Hers.*"

"Huh? Nevermind. Look, here's the deal. You give me something I can use to catch Dion and I'll turn you."

"Tonight?"

"If I catch him tonight," I answered. My fingers were crossed, so it wasn't really binding.

Hunter gave me a hard look, trying to judge if I was telling the truth, if I could be trusted. I gave him my best innocent face.

"Want me to pinky swear?" I asked. It didn't cost me anything. If the vampire myths could be believed, I didn't have a soul to soil. As long as he didn't make me swear on a stack of Bibles, I was golden.

"Fine, but I want a taste."

I'd seen what my blood could do back in New York when it healed up a goth guy who'd been beaten into a coma. Just drinking my blood wouldn't transform Hunter—there had to be a give-and-take between us, as in *you scratch my back, I'll scratch yours . . . and drink your blood.*

"Talk first."

Hunter shrugged and took a sip of his wine, forgetting to roll it around in his mouth before swallowing this time, and asked, "What do you want to know?"

"Everything. I keep hearing that Dion 'changed.' Tell me all about him, before and after."

The waitress came by to ask if we wanted another glass for me and to let us know that the kitchen would be closing in half an hour. I accepted the glass, just for appearances, but declined the menu and she went away. Hunter didn't watch her go, which would have been totally sweet if we'd been on a date. His eyes also hadn't dropped to my cleavage more than three or four times. He was a regular gentleman.

"Before the change... well, Dion was kind of a geek," he told me. *Okay*, I thought, *that was like the pot calling the kettle whacked.* "He did something with electronics, I think," Hunter went on. "And he was kind of on the fringes of the Burgess Brigade. I mean, he hung with us and all, mostly sniffing around Kali, but he never received a formal invitation to join the clan. Then he started working for Xander..."

"Wait," I cut in. "Kali? Xander? Pretend I don't have any idea what you're talking about." *Yeah, just pretend.*

"I think Kali's real name is Kelly. That was her family Dion went after. It was all over the news."

Kelly Swinter. Okay, I was with him so far. "And Xander?"

"If he's got a last name, I don't know it. He's one of them... I mean, of *you*."

Funny that Selene had left out that little piece of information about Dion's employment. I wondered how it fit in. Had Dion stolen something from the vamps, so they wanted him alive to lead them to it? Was there something he knew that they wanted to beat out of him?

"So working for Xander changed him?" I asked.

"Not at first. At first, he was still, well, *him*. Maybe a little cockier than usual."

"Because he'd taken the deal you mentioned? Servitude in exchange for the eternal kiss?"

"Yeah, and because he thought it gave him some kind

of status, working for *them*. When he disappeared, I thought the vamps were behind it. They aren't exactly out of the coffin, and there he was shooting his mouth off. Not that most people would listen, only those of us who'd figured it out. The true believers."

"*Were* they behind it?"

Hunter's eyes searched the shadowy bar as if nervous that we'd be overheard, but no one was nearby. Only Bobby, with his super-vamp hearing, was close enough to pick up the conversation from where he sat at a table that let him see both us and the door, but Hunter bypassed him given his assumptions about human hearing range.

His gaze came back to me, those moss-green eyes almost black in the low light. "I don't know. He wouldn't say anything about where he'd been when he came back, but it was like he was a different person. Arrogant instead of just cocky; driven instead of desperate; a leader instead of a follower. That was when he started spouting the crazy ideas that got him banished."

"What do you think happened to him while he was gone?"

"I don't know, but it was enough to scare the daylights out of me. Uh, no pun intended."

"It didn't scare you enough to keep you away from the club."

The look he gave me said he had no idea why it should. "That's where my people are."

"Um, okay, so when Dion went off on his own, he took others with him?"

"He'd already started ... I don't know what you'd call it. Recruiting? He talked about rising up, a blood tide, a sea of change … all kinds of crazy clichés. I tried to talk to him, but he was … I don't know, *different*. Driven. Like a man on a mission."

"So you think he was, what, possessed? Touched in the head?"

"I don't know what I think. *Something* happened to him. Whatever it was turned him into a killer."

A shiver went up my spine like a black cat had just walked over my grave, which was just silly since I wasn't even in it any more. I looked around the bar, searching for the source of the feeling, and met Selene's cold dark eyes. *Selene. Here.*

Wherever she'd come from, she had both hands on Bobby's shoulders, holding him in his seat. He hadn't sent me a mental message, so I figured it wasn't anything he couldn't handle, at least for the moment, but—

Hunter noticed my preoccupation, followed my gaze, and froze. I mean, he hadn't been all that animated before, but this was the stillness of the rabbit in the meadow, hoping the hawk wouldn't notice him. He must have recognized Selene from the club.

"Shit," he said under his breath.

I put a hand on his arm, and he flinched like I'd struck him. "Don't worry. They want me to find Dion. You've only been helping me do it."

From the white all around his eyes, he wasn't taking much comfort in that. "I've got to go. I'll take a rain check on that blood." He tried to slip out, but I was in his way. "Please," he said, his eyes meeting mine.

I took pity and let him escape.

"Join us," Selene asked, barely sparing Hunter a glance

as he fled the scene. It wasn't a question, and I didn't take it as one.

I tossed some money down on Hunter's table and went to face down Selene.

"Sit," she ordered.

"I'd rather stand, thanks."

She eyed me coldly, but I didn't take it personally. "If I'd wanted to hurt you, you'd be begging for mercy by now," she informed me. "I want a progress report. I understand you had Dion in your sights earlier tonight. You let him slip away."

"I didn't *let* him do anything," I bit out. "He had a woman hostage, an ambush waiting to spring, and a house burning down around us. It was a trap."

"Some would have chosen death before dishonor."

I put a hand on one hip and stared her down. "Yeah, introduce them to me. Anyway, if failure were a killing offense, algebra would have sent me to an early grave. I won't do you any good dead."

"I don't see that you're doing us much good alive."

We eyed each other like two lionesses about to spring for the same piece of meat ... or each others' throats if one got in the way of the other.

"Maybe that's because you've been holding out on us," I said. "If we're going to stop Dion, we're going to need to talk to Xander."

An actual expression crossed her face ... surprise, maybe. Somehow, I sensed it wasn't so much about Xander's involvement but the fact that I knew about it.

Then she closed off and was every bit as catwalk-model cold as she'd ever been. "I'm afraid that's not possible."

"Honey, we're the *living dead*. Don't tell me what's not possible."

She didn't even blink. Her game face was back in place. "Xander is ... no longer with us."

I studied her, but she was as smooth as ice that's just been zambonied. *"No longer with us* as in true dead? Gone? What?"

"Yes," she answered.

"To which?"

"For all intents and purposes, Xander is dead and gone."

"For all intents and purposes—what does that mean?"

"I'll find you a dictionary."

I growled.

"You have two nights," she said. "Then if we have to tear down this town to get to Dion and to you, so be it." I had a feeling Selene had been lobbying for that route right from the start.

"Why is this kid so important to you?" I asked.

Her hands tightened on Bobby's shoulders and I saw him bite back a wince.

"Why is he so important to *you*?" she said.

Her ice was starting to seep into my heart, and I let it come out in my voice. "I doubt our reasons are the same."

"Reasons don't matter. Only results."

She gave Bobby's shoulders a final brutal squeeze and let go.

"One last question," I said quickly, before she could disappear into the night. "How is it that you can track me, but not Dion?"

She smiled, a sphinx's grin, like right before it pounces and has you for dinner. "We have our ways."

Then she was gone, and Bobby and I were left staring at each other.

"The phone," I said into the silence. "Damn, I should have thought of that. If Sid can track us via GPS on the Fed phone, the vamps can probably do the same with the one they gave me."

I was tempted to plant it on one of the bar's patrons and be done with it, but that might put some unsuspecting person in danger. And if I just flushed it, Selene would figure it out when the phone stayed put. Anyway, it might still have a use. Right now, though, I felt like I was carrying a moving target.

As I was thinking it, the target rang in my pocket. Bobby's gaze flickered from mine to my phone. "You gonna answer that?"

Reluctantly, I pulled the phone from my pocket. "Yeah," I said into it.

"Ask your Federal friends what became of Alistaire."

Selene. She hung up before I could say a word. Weird.

Alistaire was the creepy psycho-psychic who'd dubbed me "chaos" and who'd tried alternately to end and save my life. I owed him. I didn't know for what, exactly, but I couldn't shake the feeling. He'd gone missing on Bobby's and my last mission. I'd thought he'd escaped, that the Feds had missed him, but what if…?

What if, what? Why capture him and not tell us? Were secrets just that habitual with the Feds, or was there something more sinister going on they didn't want us to know about?

9

I needed answers, and TV game shows had taught me exactly what to do in such situations—phone a friend. The problem was, I didn't think it was such a hot idea to call Marcy on a Fed-supplied phone to ask my questions. For all I knew, calls were recorded for quality assurance. Besides, Sid and Maya hadn't let me put her on speed dial, since the plan had been for me to get caught and for her to stay hidden. That meant my only option was to play telephone... with Bobby as the phone.

We got into the car with the doors firmly shut and locked around us, and I turned to him. "Bobby, ring up Marcy, would you?"

"Ring her up?"

"You know, do that voodoo you do so well. Give her a shout-out."

"O-kay. The point being?" he asked.

"She works with Brent. He's one of *them*. A Fed. Maybe she knows something or can find out. Maybe he talks in his sleep or has a map to some super-secret government facility tattooed on his ass. I don't know."

"You want her to check out his butt?"

"Honey, if I know Marcy, she already has."

His mouth opened and closed for a second like a landed fish. You'd have thought he'd be used to me by now. I was glad I could still surprise him.

"Whatever," he said finally. "But I don't want details."

I rolled my eyes. "Fine."

"Drive," Bobby ordered.

"I want to give the call my full focus."

"We're sitting ducks here. I'd rather be on the move."

He had a point. "Okay then, where to?" I asked.

"Back to HQ, but look for tails and make sure not to take a direct route."

"But the vamps can find me anywhere, any time they want."

"They're not the only ones we're worried about."

True enough. I told him what Selene had said about Alistaire as I put the car into gear and pulled out of the space I'd backed into for a quick getaway. I hadn't really thought beyond relief that the psycho-psychic hadn't darkened my door since our last case, but now that I thought about things, it was out of character for him not to turn up again like a bad penny.

Sure, vampires could be killed … just like humans, only different. But Alistaire was something infinitely scarier.

"And you think this means—what?" Bobby asked.

I stared at him until he grabbed the steering wheel to yank us back into our lane, then I switched over to words.

"She said it like something had happened to Alistaire and that the Feds were responsible."

"This is Alistaire we're talking about. Do you really think the spooks can out-boogey the boogeyman?"

"I don't know," I said, "but I mean to find out. I told you all along that something was off. This just confirms it."

It was Bobby's turn to stare. "It doesn't confirm anything. You're not saying the *vamps* are suddenly reliable sources of information now?"

I shot him a look. Just quickly this time, because I was in no mood to die. "Careful, *we're* vamps."

"You know what I mean."

"Actually, I don't. You seem very cozy with the Feds lately, like maybe you've been drinking their brand of Kool-Aid. Have you ever noticed there are no vampire handlers? I haven't seen any vampires in charge, have you?"

Bobby bit his lip while he thought about that. "No," he said at last.

"Right, so we check in with Marcy?"

In answer, Bobby closed his eyes and I felt that ripple of power from him, like someone had electrified the air. It made me all tingly.

"Hey, Marcy," he said aloud for my benefit. All he really had to do to mind-speak to Marcy was think. "Wait, wait,

wait, slow down." Then, to me, "She wants you to call her, something about an awesome dress in clockwork orange."

"Ooh, ask her if it's red-orange or closer to copper, because she should totally stay away from the more yellowy tones."

"Gina wants to know—wait a minute, what am I doing? Girls, *focus*. Criminal investigation, remember? Marcy, there's something weird going on. I don't know if the vamps are just yanking our chains, but they've implicated the Feds in at least one vampire disappearance. We don't know if the Feds have some kind of Guantanamo Bay for the undead or—" He paused. "*Guan-tan-a-mo*," he repeated. "Not Geronimo. G-u-a-…Look, forget it. We want you to see if you can get any information out of Brent."

Pause.

"She says he's not there right now."

"Well, where is he?" I asked.

He passed it along.

"Where? But he's left some things behind, right? Things you can go through for clues." Another pause. "Like, I don't know…anything. Check his computer."

Bobby started to bang his head against the window. I knew the feeling. Marcy could make you nuts like that. I wondered if shatter-resistant glass was built to withstand the undead.

"Okay, let us know if you find anything," he said. "I'll tell her. Bye."

"Tell me what?" I asked.

"It blows Betsy Carmichael's dress out of the water…that mean anything to you?"

"It means she damn well better take pictures!" Of the dress anyway, since she, sadly, wouldn't show.

"Shoot me now," he said. "I wonder if the Feds make vampire-strength migraine meds."

"You can ask them yourself; we're almost there." In fact, I was turning onto our street now. "It's your own fault, anyway. If you hadn't—"

Our street was apparently the latest crime scene. At least there was no ambulance, although a police patrol unit lit up the storefront with alternating flashes of red and blue. The bullet-proof windows of the pawnshop were still intact, but it looked like the door had been ripped off its hinges; it now canted to the left like a bird's broken wing.

And inside, a uniformed officer stood with Sid and Maya, a guy I figured was the pawnshop frontman, and—*Brent*. At least, I thought it was him. He was the right size and build, but he didn't currently look like a Fed *or* a goth. He looked like any frat boy off the street—baseball cap pulled low over his face, cargo shorts, gray sweatshirt.

I cruised right on past, hoping that they wouldn't see me. I parked on a side street two blocks away.

"Do we check it out?" I asked Bobby, as though he actually had a choice in the matter.

"Yeah," he said. "I think we'd better."

We strolled back toward the shop under the cover of darkness and stopped behind a clutch of palm trees a half block away, outside the reach of the flashing red and blues. In the doorway, we could see Sid and Maya shaking the officer's hand and sending him on his way with a "Thank you, officer. We'll fax over a full list of what's been taken after we've done inventory."

The words carried to our sharpened senses, but with all

the crap in the window, we couldn't see well enough into the store to check out what the others were up to. *Closer*, I said mentally, hoping Bobby would pick up on it. I don't know why I bothered—human senses weren't as accurate as ours. I could have whispered and they'd never have heard, but it was getting harder to remember being human.

Bobby gave me a nod. We waited for Sid and Maya to go back inside the store, waited for the patrol unit's lights to go out and the car to drive off. Then we made our move, crossing the street, avoiding the security and street lights, and making it to the corner of the pawnshop/HQ building. We peeked through the front window, finding a gap between a poster for an antique weapons show and an old toaster oven. Inside, the new player in our little dramedy, the pawnbroker, was showing Brent a wall safe. We could only see Brent in profile, but he had one hand inside the vault and his eyes were closed as if he was concentrating.

Then I felt the wash of power. Not a tsunami like Bobby's, but more the natural flow of the ocean. Still, it was enough to make the hair on my arms stand on end. And it wasn't coming from me—as far as I could tell, my only superpowers were magical sensitivity and resistance to mesmerism. Oh, and *chaos*. Yeah, the thing with that is it doesn't come when you call. And just try putting it on your resume.

"What's he doing?" I whispered to Bobby.

Bobby's eyes were shining, as electric blue as I'd ever seen them and completely focused on the scene inside. "He's reading the vault," he whispered back. "Brent must be a telemetric. It makes sense why he'd be part of our team. I'd wondered—"

The dead weight of my heart sank to my stomach. I

sometimes forgot we vamps hadn't cornered the market on magic. Just by touching your plate, a telemetric could tell you what you had for dinner and whether you used your finger to push the last of the peas onto your fork. More usefully, he could probably tell who'd been in the vault and maybe even where they were headed afterward.

So, we had a telemetric on our side and the Tampa vamps had a truth-teller on theirs. Two truly *powerful* powers. Right here. There was definitely more going on than some killer kids. *Way* more, if both sides had brought out the big guns. I hoped Bobby and I weren't caught in the crossfire.

Crap! *Marcy.* If Brent could read objects, could he read people as well? If so, one touch and he'd find out we'd asked Marcy to spy on him. He'd know we had suspicions about what the Feds were up to. We'd be totally exposed.

"Bobby, you have to tell Marcy."

"Shh!" Bobby hissed.

I was about to get all indignant when I realized he was trying to listen in on Brent's report.

"Why didn't you pass this machine along right away?" Brent was asking.

The pawnshop guy crossed his arms defensively. "Hadn't had time to investigate it yet. We've let it be known we're in the market for the unusual and the occult. Do you know how many crazy stories we get? If I passed them all along, you guys would be chasing your tails day and night. When a guy comes in saying he's got an energy transference machine, I take his name, give him a few bucks, and send him on his way. Business as usual."

"Until now," Sid cut in.

Pawn guy looked just shy of mutinous when a flash of … something around the far corner of the shop caught my attention. I squinted into the night, trying to catch it again.

There it was—a quick glint of light reflecting off glass … no, *glasses*. We weren't the only eavesdroppers. I was torn between sneaking up on our Peeping Tom or staying to listen in, but then realized I could pretty much be in two places at once.

Stay here, I ordered Bobby. I'd get the full scoop later, probably word for word. He had that kind of memory. Meanwhile, I crept silently toward the corner, but not close enough to the building that I'd set off any potential perimeter alarms. I peered around. Nothing.

Apparently, I wasn't stealthy enough. When I peeked around the corner where the Peeping Tom had disappeared, I found him staring right at me. Yes, *he*—brown wavy hair tending toward frizz, wild eyebrows that did their best to meet up with his hairline, round glasses sliding down his nose. Fine lines and wrinkles put him at about my dad's age, give or take. He held a finger to his lips, signaling me to be silent—as if I hadn't been. When he took it away, he mouthed, "Trust no one."

Then he bolted like a rabbit. There one second, gone the next. Like magic … literally. I felt it like a backdraft sizzling over me. I knew there wasn't any point in giving chase and possibly calling attention to myself. He was *gone*. Just gone.

I circled back around to Bobby. "I missed him," I said when I got close, "but I got a decent look. Three guesses who it was." Our Peeping Tom looked just like his picture in the Fed's briefing folder.

"Batman?" Bobby asked. "Santa Claus? The missing uncle?"

I stared. "How did you know?"

"Men's intuition."

"Men don't get to have intuition."

He rolled his eyes at me. "Okay, fine, I was guessing."

"Well anyway, you're right. It was Eric Ricci—checking on one of his inventions, maybe. I mean, an energy transference machine sounds right up his alley."

"But why? And how did it get here in the first place?"

"Your guess is as good as mine. If I'd caught him, we could have asked. Selene only gave us two more nights to find the killer kids, and so far we keep finding more questions and no answers. Ideas?"

Bobby shrugged. "I guess we go on in. If Sid's tracking us with GPS, he'll know we stopped here. Might as well own it. We can tell him we were chasing after their Peeping Tom."

"And the fact that we let him get away?"

"We sort of gloss over that part."

"Works for me."

Bobby offered me his arm, and together we strolled toward the open door of the No Name Pawnshop.

We entered just in time to hear Brent say, "It's like they purposely blanked their minds, somehow. They made sure to leave no trace—"

He stopped as soon as he saw us, and the others turned as well.

"So glad you could join us," Sid said wryly. He had his poker face on, so it was impossible to tell what he thought about our sudden appearance.

"We were in the neighborhood," Bobby answered. "What happened here?"

"Break in."

"I can see that. Details?"

Everyone exchanged looks, and finally Sid said, "Some electronics were stolen. No big deal, really. But this close to headquarters, while we're conducting a mission … it pays to be suspicious. We check everything out."

Uh huh. He was definitely hiding something. Bobby and I exchanged a look of our own.

"Well, you're not the only ones checking things out," Bobby told him. "You had an audience. We chased him off—"

"Chased him off? You didn't think to bring him in for questioning?"

"Where? Right here at HQ? Or maybe we should have turned him over to the cops?"

Oh, good going, Bobby—deflection. I was so proud of my boy.

"I got a good look at him, though," I said, jumping in with more distraction. "You'll never guess who it was."

"Well, don't keep us in suspense," Sid snapped.

I let the moment build. One beat. Two. Until Sid looked like he was grinding his teeth to nubs. "Eric Ricci. Nelson's uncle," I told him, in my best dramatic voice.

The silence was golden.

Sid turned to Brent. "Any chance you can track him?"

Brent shot me a look, then Bobby, before saying clearly less than he meant. "I can try."

On Sid's order, I took Brent around to the side of the building where I'd seen the mad inventor, and once I pointed out where he'd stood, what he'd touched, etc., Brent shooed me on my way, back to the others.

But I refused to be shooed.

"What?" he asked, when I didn't vamoose.

"I want to watch and learn," I answered, all innocence.

"Well, you can't."

"Why not?"

"I need to be distraction-free. I need to focus."

"You won't even know I'm here."

He ground his teeth together and I wondered if the Feds had a dental plan … for his sake and Sid's. "Yes," he said through the clenched teeth, "I will."

"Fine, then. I'm out." I turned to go, but stopped and spun to face him again. "Just one more thing while I have you alone. I don't know what's between you and Marcy, but if you hurt my friend, you answer to me."

He looked sad for a second. "I don't think that's going to be a problem."

"Why? Because there's nothing there or because you won't hurt her?"

"Yes."

"Yes, what?"

"All of it. Now, will you *please* let me work?"

"Who's stopping you?"

This time I went. Back to the others. Back to secrets and more questions than we had answers for. To debriefing and dodging and eventually, hopefully, showering.

I smelled like a crematorium. Burning flesh and blood. Which made me think of the girl we'd left behind in the burning house and whether she'd lived to tell the tale. I hadn't been able to see clearly, but from the amount of hair I'd had to brush aside, I guessed it was Kelly. My dead heart clenched. Maybe Sid, with all his contacts and mad computer skillz, could find out whether her body had been found—whether she'd burned up in the fire or miraculously, mysteriously survived. I knew it was false hope, but I couldn't help it. It was the only thing keeping me going.

On second thought, maybe I didn't want to know the truth. In the end, I didn't say a word as we all trooped through the pawnshop to the heavily reinforced connecting door to HQ.

10

I was still in the shower when I heard a noise like an electric razor starting up and realized it was my phone ... my *Fed* phone ... on vibrate, rattling on the counter as it did when I had a call or message coming in. Immediately, I thought of Marcy and bolted out of the shower, soap in my eyes and dripping all over the floor, to grab for the phone. In all the insanity of spying on the spies and then debriefing, I hadn't had the chance to call and tell her about Brent's ability until, well, shower time, when I'd completely forgotten about it in my quest for clean.

But all that awaited me was a text from *Restricted*. Baffled, I clicked over to the message, which sent ice racing through my veins.

Check out the "closed" Sun State Clinic on
Mercer. Come alone. Tell no one.

A Friend

The message mysteriously erased itself as I read.

I couldn't even form a thought beyond *Huh?* Except for Hunter and the Feds, no one had this number, and while any of them might call from a restricted number, no one I knew had the power or know-how to erase the words as they were read. Sid might have the technical knowledge to retract a text, but the timing... that smacked of magic, and Sid was most definitely a mundane. Or the best actor in the known world.

I debated what to do. At some point—tonight, even—I should probably go back to my apartment and play bait for the killer kids, but that would give me only the illusion of freedom. The Feds would probably have some kind of surveillance on my place so they could close in if the kids showed, which meant I'd be watched.

And speaking of traps, the text could very well be one—the Feds testing my loyalty, seeing if I'd keep secrets from them. Or it could be the killer kids trying to lure me out on my own. So, going somewhere on the basis of an anonymous text would be stupid. Too many unknowns. But *not* going... not even an option. I was way, way too curious. Plus, it might matter to the mission. Plus again, the sooner we wrapped this up, the sooner I got back to the downtime I loved so much—*Project Runway*, mani-pedis, slipping off with Bobby. No uncontrollable thirst, raging fires, killer kids, or vampire truth-tellers.

Okay, so I was going to follow the lead. Like that had really ever been in question. But the trick was to go smart ... and I just happened to have an idea about that.

I dressed quickly, brushed, flipped, fluffed, dabbed, the whole nine yards. Then I went to pitch my cover story to the Feds. I told them I needed to get back to my place to play bait. The killer kids had come for me there once before and left me that lovely wall art. Maybe if I went home, I argued, they'd try again.

All this because I knew I couldn't leave for my rendezvous straight from HQ. Sid and Maya wouldn't even need to have me followed—my cell phone GPS would give me away. If I "accidentally" left my phone at HQ, someone might stop by my place to return it and I'd be discovered missing. I wouldn't put it past them; Sid seriously hated anyone being out of communication range for even an instant. The Feds disappeared people who crossed them, or so I'd heard. I didn't want to find out firsthand.

If they hadn't set all hands on deck to research the latest known cult member, I'm not sure they'd have let me leave, but I was a proven disaster at research, chasing one bright, shiny tangent after another. It was a lot like doing dishes. Break a few plates the first time ... or crash one little computer system ... and no one asks you to do it again.

I wondered whether they'd send Bobby home with me as backup, but he was a research whiz and couldn't be spared. Besides, I think Sid and Maya thought we might get a little ... distracted ... with the place all to ourselves, and miss the signs of any danger at my door. So I was on my own, just like I'd hoped. Not that I didn't want Bobby as backup for the rendezvous, but if my anonymous texter didn't show because I'd brought Bobby along, I'd miss out on whatever he or she had to tell me. If it was a trap, I had a way better chance of rescue if Bobby was on the outside rather than inside with me.

Sid and Maya did, however, order me up some watchdogs, as anticipated. They arrived within a half hour of plan approval, one of them driving the car I'd been issued and which the Feds had towed away for examination after the home invasion. The other bodyguard drove a nondescript black car with tinted windows. The first guy unfolded himself from my car and kept going, all six and a half feet of him. He then climbed into the passenger seat of the other car, leaving me to adjust my mirrors and seats, the angle of the steering wheel, the air conditioning vents, you name it.

I drove home, constantly looking in my rearview window, but my surveillance team was good. They even took a different route back to my place so that no one would see them following me. While I was alone, I grabbed my vamp-supplied cell and dialed Hunter; I could have speed-dialed him on the Fed phone, but I couldn't be sure the Feds weren't recording my calls. And Hunter's number was full of nines and sixes and totally easy to remember.

Even with ninja-vamp reflexes, driving while dialing was probably not recommended by the highway patrol. But I only got flipped off once, and it was totally her own fault that she didn't realize a yellow light meant speed up, not slow the hell down. And anyway, I missed her by an eyelash.

Hunter showed up at my door twenty minutes after me with Mina in tow, just as I'd asked. She had her hair rolled into a French twist, also as I'd asked, since there was no better way to hide the fact that I had a helluva lot more hair than she did.

I'd entered my apartment as Gina Covello, or Gail Kuttner, or whoever, but I was leaving as Mina Whatshername. I hoped her shoes were my size.

I greeted them at the door with a kiss to both cheeks so that my bodyguards could see me, and then I ushered them inside.

Mina's eyes were gleaming. "Hunter filled me in."

I cut my gaze to his. "Only what I know," he swore, "which isn't much."

"Better for you that way," I answered, cool and cryptic.

I hadn't told him where I was going or why. Just that I needed to escape my apartment without being seen. If he thought that was weird, he kept it to himself.

"Come on," I said to Mina. "Let's switch clothes."

"Right here?" she asked.

Hunter looked a little too interested in that idea.

"My room," I said, taking her hand.

"Hey, I should get something out of this," he protested. "At least you could let me watch."

"You get to imagine," I told him. "Stay."

Hunter pouted like a little boy denied dessert, and Mina said, too close to my ear, "I want to hear all about it when you get back."

"Sure, I could tell you, but then I'd have to kill you."

"Oh please, is that the best you can do?"

"No, but it's not the worst, either." I turned and let a little of the night's darkness seep into my eyes, and she shuddered, but I wasn't sure it was in fear.

Once in the bedroom, I shut the door and quickly

stripped. She watched, which was a little freaky. "Uh, I need your clothes," I reminded her.

"Oh, right." She wore a wrap dress, so all she had to do was untie the knot at her hip and unwrap it. It was also aqua. Good for drawing the eye and focusing attention away from the face. Lousy for sneaking around at night. But since I'd be waltzing right out the front door, there was no sneakage required.

"What size are your feet?" I asked.

"Six and a half."

"Close enough." I wanted to be as complete in my transformation as possible. I didn't know the watchdogs outside or how observant they might be, but if borrowed shoes had meant hobbling around like a wicked stepsister trying to fit into Cinderella's size-five glass slippers, I'd have opted for my own kicks.

I stepped into her shoes and twirled in the dress. "How do I look?" I asked.

"Great. Just keep your face out of the light, stand as tall as you can, and hope no one notices our height difference."

"It's not all that much!" I protested.

"Honey, if you have lifts stashed away somewhere, now would be a good chance to use them."

Finished, I texted Bobby one word—*Listen*—hoping he'd understand and that no one else who might be reading his messages would, then locked my two phones away in a drawer. I traded out the contents of my purse for Mina's.

"Ready," I announced.

"Really, you're not even going to give me a hint what you're up to?"

"Not a one."

"Tease."

I shrugged. "Not the worst I've been called. I promise, I'll make it worth your while."

"That's what they all say."

"I'm *so* not like everyone else."

"They say that too."

"Whatever. I have to go."

I went to the door and she followed me back to the living room.

"Wow," Hunter said as we stepped out. "You two could be sisters."

"I was going for twins, but I'll take what I can get," I answered wryly. "You ready?"

He stood, and I suddenly realized that he'd been sitting on the poisoned couch. Of course, it had been cleaned by crime scene pros at federal expense, and anyway, he was human, so the holy water wouldn't have hurt him, but it made me realize that leaving Mina here wasn't a simple bait and switch. I was putting her in danger. There were watchdogs out front, and I could hope the killer kids had done enough damage for one night, but—

"Hold on a minute."

I went into the kitchen and chose the biggest knife I could out of the butcher block. I supposed that if I cooked I'd actually know what it was for, but anyway it looked big enough to butcher a pig...or a person. I came back and tucked it between two of the couch cushions.

"Just in case," I told her.

"In case of what?"

"Murderers, thieves, things that go bump in the night… Anyone who comes through that door who isn't us."

"You really know how to put your guests at ease."

"I don't want you at ease. I want you on guard. Um, enjoy."

She looked at me doubtfully, and I couldn't blame her. I wasn't even sure I had cable. I took Hunter's arm and we went on our way, but not without a worried glance back. Mina, however, already seemed to have forgotten her concerns and sat back against the couch cushions to prop her feet up on my coffee table, TV remote in hand.

I was careful as we left to keep my face in shadow, turned almost into Hunter's neck as I pretended to talk his ear off, stretching myself to be as tall as possible. Hunter helped by leaning in to listen to my pretend monologue. It was a relief to get to his car without incident. He started it and took off, slowly to avoid suspicion.

"You brought the spare clothes?" I asked.

"In the back."

I kicked off Mina's shoes and dove for the back seat.

"So, what's this all about, and where am I taking you?" he asked, only keeping his eyes on the road every few seconds. The rest of the time he spent watching the rearview mirror.

"I told you I can't tell you that."

"I thought that was just for Mina. As your human servant…"

"You're *not* my human servant."

"But I could be."

I hated to burst his bubble, especially when his fondest wish was to be my minion, so I left it alone.

"Anyway," he added, "you'll at least have to tell me *where* we're going so I can get us there."

"You know the old clinic on Mercer?"

"The one that's half burnt out?"

"I'm guessing that's the one."

"But why? It's deserted."

I gave him a *look*.

"Yeah, yeah, I know, 'then you'd have to kill me,'" he said. "But if you need backup—"

"I don't."

"Whatever."

I smiled. That was my line. While we'd been talking, I'd pulled out the clothes I'd asked for, which were way more appropriate to night-stalking—black jeans, black long-sleeved T-shirt, tennies.

"You're lucky my little sister just went through a goth phase," Hunter said, his gaze temporarily on the road. "If you'd wanted, I could have gotten you all the leather and chains you could handle."

I wrinkled my nose. Been there, done that, wasn't allowed to keep the T-shirt. I wasn't a big fan of message tees, but *Bite Me* was right for so many occasions.

"Thanks anyway. Creaking and clanking really aren't my style."

"I figured."

We turned onto Mercer ten minutes later. I was all suited up in cat-burglar chic.

"That gas station over there," I said, nodding to the right about a block up the road. "Is it close to the clinic?"

"Maybe half a mile."

"Good, you can wait for me there."

"But—"

"I was told to come alone, and that's what I plan to do."

Okay, so sneakers have their uses. For one, they have the word "sneak" right in them, so they put you straight into stealth mode. For another, they're not nearly as cute as wedges or boots or stilettos, so you're less concerned about getting blood all over them. You don't want to be thinking about your footwear replacement costs in the midst of battle. It's a distraction that can get you killed.

Here's the only problem... they're no protection against a hungry gator. But then, what is? I only hoped I didn't meet up with one. There was a patch of grass along the side of the road, maybe two or three feet wide, and then an overgrown mess of weedy forest that looked like it could reach out and grab the unwary. Trees dripped with Spanish moss; prickly thorn bushes camouflaged themselves with pretty little flowers. I wasn't going to think about the wildlife they might be hiding in there. Spiders and snakes and... Nope, those thoughts were going into the psychic shredder, along with all the other things I couldn't bear to face, like Kelly Swinter's fate. Someday my pent-up paranoias would explode on me. I just hoped I wasn't doing anything life threatening when it happened.

But for now, I'd brave the wild growth. It was the only way to sneak up on the clinic and get the lay of the land before committing. It felt like some kind of cosmic justice for what I'd done to Kelly each time a thorn gashed my arm or I stepped into a swamp—which totally described, like, half the state of Florida. Yeah, because the universe punished murder with petty torment. Or, maybe not so petty if any of the stingers or fangs I feared got ahold of me.

This was me, *not* thinking about it.

I had to circle around behind a small strip mall complex and then, finally, the clinic. I assumed so, anyway, based on Hunter's description of it as half-burnt. Huge wooden walls were erected around the building, half hiding it from view. I'd seen the same thing on umpteen construction projects in my life, but never before topped with razor-wire. In the yard hemmed in by the fence, a crane stood silent against the night. That was about all I could see from my position. As I'd known all along, I was just going to have to go in.

I heard something move in the growth behind me, and that helped get me moving. I pictured huge venomous teeth ... snake, gator, it hardly mattered. I was so out of there. I slid out of the woods and began to circle the wooden wall at a decent distance, in case there were any proximity alarms or the like. The wall was solid. No knots or warps in the wood to peek through. Three quarters of the way around there was a parking lot, mostly hidden from the road by the bulk of the clinic. There were four cars in it, which seemed odd in an abandoned building with the construction stopped for the night. There was also a door in the wall—padlocked, of course—leading from the lot to the clinic yard.

The heebie-jeebies danced across my skin. I didn't know what this place was yet, but something about it freaked me out worse than the possible snakes in the grass. There was definitely something unnatural about the place. I didn't know what gave it away—maybe the razor wire or wall-mounted video cameras. Both made me *very* curious what someone was so determined to protect.

"You made it," a voice said out of the darkness.

I whipped my head around to the right and saw a man standing there, just, I thought, out of camera range, looking all absent-minded professor. *Eric Ricci—my mystery texter?*

"The Feds have been looking for you," I said, hushed, since I didn't know what other security the clinic might have in place ... guards, dogs, whatever.

"Everybody has," he answered. "But I'm only interested in one person ... my nephew."

Wow, I so didn't know how to break it to him. "Um, you do know he's wanted by the police, right? For murder."

He was shaking his head in denial before my sentence had fully formed. "That's not him."

"It sure looks like him. He's been positively identified."

"Not *him*," Eric insisted. "Someone's wearing Nelson's face and body, but the boy I knew is gone. I want you to find him."

"I don't mean to sound dense, but ... huh?"

"I raised that boy from a toddler. I *know* him. Whoever that is, isn't him. And the worst is, it's all my fault."

"You've totally lost me."

Ever have one of those nightmares where you're onstage, spotlight on you, and even though everyone else knows their lines, you don't even know what part you're playing? This felt just like that.

He huffed. "The machine taken from the pawnshop ... it transfers energy."

"Okay, I'm with you so far."

"There was another machine, a companion piece if you

will, that transfers consciousness—like a brain transplant without the risky surgery and chance of organ rejection. Just imagine the potential for psychology, politics, negotiation ... Someone could literally walk a mile in someone else's shoes. But they used Nelson to get it. And, I'm afraid, as their first test subject."

"Okay, pretend I'm not riding the crazy train with you," I said, resisting the urge to back away slowly. "I hate to say it, but, um, your inventions don't work. You couldn't have had anything to do with whatever's happened to Nelson. I've been to your place and seen the letters—"

"Lies!" he cried, going from mild-mannered professor to psycho in zero to sixty. His eyes flamed supernova and his body language went suddenly aggressive, as if he'd like to grab me by my shoulders and shake sense into me—hard. "Those idiots at the Patent Office. They can't see the genius, the vision. Just because *they* can't make them work ... or so they say. Anyway, *someone* recognized my genius. Someone close enough to make a play for the consciousness transfer device."

"What makes you think Nelson had anything to do with it?"

"He started acting strangely ... just before. Cockier, more furtive—not himself, but not in the way he's not himself now. One day, just like any other, we were home alone. I was working on my machines. I heard the door open behind me, and then, suddenly, I was out like a light."

"Inner or outer door?"

"What? I don't know. I was lucky to remember my own name. I woke up somewhere strange, disoriented like I'd been drugged or my brain was boggled. Somehow, I escaped. I barely remember getting home, but when I did, both Nelson and the consciousness transference device were gone. I grabbed what I could and ran."

Wow, so many questions, so little time. "Was anything else missing besides your nephew and your brain-swap thingie?"

He looked furtively left and right, as if to make sure the trees weren't listening in. "That came later. I decided to pawn the energy transference machine and kind of put the word out on the street. I thought that whoever had the first device might come for the second. I thought I could flush out whoever it was Nelson was mixed up with, and track them to him."

"And?"

He grabbed my arm, trying to convey his need. The touch made my skin prickle. At first I thought it was goose bumps, but then I realized it was *power*. Every time Bobby used his telekinesis or other mental mojo, and when Brent had "read" the vault, I'd felt a similar tingle. But Eric's power was different from either of theirs—unfocused, almost raw and wild. Not like a wave, more like a live wire. I wondered if *he* was aware of it.

Speaking of focus, I had to get back on track. Daylight would come far too soon. "So, you think someone else is walking around in Nelson's shoes?" This I could identify with.

"I know it. I've been staking out that club he always disappeared to, as well as the pawnshop, but there's only one of me. I can't be in two places at once; I have to sleep sometime."

All very interesting, edging on cuckoo-bananas, but I didn't see how any of that put us in the middle of the woods just a couple of hours before dawn.

"And this place?"

He released my gaze long enough to look at the burnt-out clinic and back.

"You have to promise me something first," he said.

"What?"

"I found this for you. You have to find him for me."

I so wished someone would hand me a script. "Great, you found it. I didn't know it was lost. *But what is it?*"

"You know animal testing—cosmetics, cancer cures, sugar substitutes?"

I nodded. I had a conscience. I might get some of my beauty out of a bottle, but not one with products first tested on cute fuzzy bunnies.

"Well, this"—he lowered his voice and looked around stealthily, even though we'd already have been caught if anyone were listening—"is a supernatural testing facility."

My mind was officially blown. "Come again? And how do you know any of this?"

"I found it when I was looking for my nephew. I figured that if someone was walking around in Nelson's skin, *Nelson* had to be somewhere else. He was in so tight with the vampires—"

"Humans pretending to be vampires," I cut in, hoping to keep the secret.

He gave me a look that said *he* wasn't stupid, but the jury was still out on me. "I thought that too, at first. Now I know better. Anyway, I knew that if anyone had Nelson, it was *them*," he continued. "I put a watch on the Tower, but I wasn't the only one watching. One day, I saw one of the young vamps kidnapped. I followed his trace here."

"Kidnapped by who?"

"I think you know."

Well, crap on a crispy, crumbly, craptastic cracker. *The Feds?*

"This," I said very clearly, just to be sure, "is a facility where testing is done on vampires?"

"Not just vampires."

My knees nearly buckled. What else was there? I mean, aside from telemetrics like Brent and people who could make books bleed, like my goth friend Bram from New York once said he'd seen … Crap, there was a whole magical world out there I'd never really thought about. I'd been so busy becoming a vamp and fighting for my un-life that I'd never really questioned things. Were there really such things as werewolves? Shifters? Fairies?

"And it's run by the Feds?" I continued, my brain still unable to grasp what he was saying.

"Look for yourself. That's why I've brought you here. First, you see what they're up to. Then you go deeper. You find Nelson for me, and I'll tell you anything you could possibly need to know."

Need to know—it always came back to that.

Eric tapped his pocket in an oddly purposeful movement, then *poof*, he was gone. Again. Just like at the pawnshop. I whirled around, looking, listening, waiting to spot the tell-tale motion of tree branches swinging back into place or to hear the crash of footfalls, but there was *nothing*.

It was like someone had just ended his transmission. Had he really even been here, or had he been more like Princess Leia in the little robot guy's memory? And yes, it scared me that I remembered more from that movie than Han in his tight pants and open-necked shirt. Either way, some of the mad scientist's inventions clearly worked, because outside of a Vegas magic show, I'd never seen anyone vanish into thin air before.

11

There I stood, all alone in the dark night, about to break into a building that should be deserted but wasn't. It might be fire-damaged or condemned. It was most certainly dangerous.

I debated waiting until tomorrow night when I could return with a man and a plan. Bobby'd proven himself a whiz kid at breaking and entering in the past; I could totally break, and probably enter, though not necessarily without getting caught. But I was becoming a little too reliant on my boy toy. I wasn't in the market for dependence. No matter what the sales tag said or how cute the packaging, dependence was like a lifetime subscription … you just paid and paid.

No, I needed to do this on my own, to prove I could

totally *own* a solo and wasn't just kept around for background beautification. This Everybody Wants Bobby thing was understandable. Hell, *I* wanted the boy. But the longer this mission went on, the more I realized that I was done with being bait, done with being dispensable and with playing entourage, the pawn of vampires and Feds. It was starting to make me forget who I was: Gina flippin' Covello, Queen of the Glammed.

I could do this. Maybe. Probably. *Definitely*. Failure was not an option.

I took a deep breath and studied the wall in front of me. I had seen a chained and padlocked entrance onto the grounds near the parking lot, but no doubt that would be the most closely monitored. So it looked like I'd be going over the wall, razor wire and all. I thought for a minute about taking off my shirt and throwing it over the wire, but I was pretty sure the light of the moon reflecting off my lily-white skin would give me away to anyone walking the perimeter. Although the sight of a half-dressed girl nearly glowing in the moonlight might be distraction enough for me to find a way past.

I approached the wall, praying I wouldn't set off any proximity alarms or disrupt any laser beams or whatever. Hopefully, with as much wildlife as they probably got out here, motion detectors and the like would be too much trouble. If I had tripped anything, I couldn't hear it. With my luck, that probably only meant the alarms were silent.

Close now, I rapped on the wall with my knuckles, only to have a metallic sort of sound come back to me, like the wood was just a façade over sheet metal. I walked a few feet and tried again, in case I'd encountered a lone dumpster or something on the other side of the wall with my first knock. My second was no better. Darn, then. Climbing and razor wire it was. The surveillance cameras wouldn't catch me, of course, but they'd totally spot any smooshing of the wire, so I had to be really, really careful.

And yet, I had to be fast. In, out, and back to my place before dawn fried me to a crisp. Nothing like a challenge.

I backed up several steps, did some stretches to limber up—my old gym teacher would have been so proud—took a deep breath out of habit, and ran at the wall. Two feet out, I gathered my tennies beneath me and leapt for all I was worth, aiming for the very top. What I really wanted was the ability to leap tall walls in a single bound, like some kind of super heroine—Fangtastic Girl or Chic Chick or something. The costume would come with some kick-ass boots for me. Maybe a bustier for Bobby's enjoyment.

What really happened was that I landed hard, hands closing on *pain*, fighting the need to release the biting blades. My knees banged against the wood; my feet scrabbled against the barrier as I fought to pull them up under me. I didn't look too fangtastic flailing around on that wall, blowing in the breeze like the cape I wouldn't have on *my* super suit. Finally, one foot caught long enough for me to push myself up until I crouched on the wall, crushing wire. I could release the barbs I'd been holding onto, but they continued to do their job, tearing chunks out of my palms, bringing blood and flesh with them as I mercilessly pulled back. I was going to leave behind enough DNA to tag me if my point of entry was discovered. Unless...I didn't know how it worked for vamps, being technically dead. Would my blood spoil as soon as it was out of my body, decompose as if I had really died at death? Did blood go bad, or did it keep like fine wine and Twinkies? Eww, two things that never should have occurred to me in the same sentence. Anyway, I was hoping for instant spoilage, like the dust to dust of Buffy-verse vamps.

I licked the blood off my own hands, squicked out even as I did it but there was no point wasting blood or leaving a trail for someone to follow. As the wounds started to close, hurting like a thousand paper cuts, I gathered myself and jumped to the ground.

"What do you think?" a voice came out of nowhere, approaching. There were no trees to duck behind. Nothing but the metal sheeting up against the wooden walls, and not enough space between them for me. I faded back into the shadows. "Think it's another of those turkey vultures?"

"Wish they'd just let us electrify the wiring and be done with it. Barbeque one bird and the rest will stay away, I guarantee you that."

"Can't … liability," his friend snorted. "What if some kid tried to climb in, looking for a place to party?"

They were just inches away from me now. The Pyro, as I decided to call the fry boy who wanted to burn the birds, unhooked a flashlight the size of a telescope from his belt and shone it at the razor wire where I'd just been. I wondered what he was compensating for with a light that size, but I decided I really didn't want to know.

"Well, we got somethin'," he said. "Blood. And I think some tissue as well. No feathers."

"Fur?"

The flashlight beam moved left and right.

"Nope." Pyro's voice was suddenly hard-edged, and I knew they'd just figured out this was no routine run or false alarm.

"I'll call it in."

Well, *darn*. I'd have to take down Pyro and his pal. Faster than the security dude could unclip his walkie-talkie, I flew out of the shadows, aiming a roundhouse kick at his chest. Something crunched—the walkie-talkie, I hoped, and not a rib—and he went down like a sacked quarterback.

"Holy shit!" Pyro shouted, swinging his flashlight my way like a police baton. It was certainly big enough. I kicked it out of his hand, dropped, whirled, and took his feet out from under him. He fell to the ground but landed on his back, legs up in the air, scissoring to catch me in the knee. I started to buckle and he caught me again, this time with a heel to the other shin. I dropped and rolled for the light I'd kicked out of his hand and came up swinging. The thing was as heavy as a metal pipe. Between that and my super-vamp strength, I was going to have to be careful not to cave in his skull.

It turned out not to be a problem. The flashlight was grabbed out of my hand by the first guy, who'd recovered from my boot to his chest. Crap!

He brought the flashlight crashing down on me instead. Oh, I saw the light—a comic book *KAPOW* flash exploded my vision into a night's sky full of stars and little else—but I knew where he'd been a second ago, and I was fast enough to take advantage. I launched myself at him, shoulder aimed just above the belt buckle, at the soft part of his stomach. He *oophed* and crumpled over me, at which point I used his momentum to toss him on top of Pyro, who was scrambling to his aid.

My vision started to clear as they went down in a big puppy pile, tangling limbs when Guy Two tried to catch Guy One before they collided. It was precious, really. I grabbed the zip-tie cuffs off their belts before they could recover and got their hands under control. Then I removed their talkies and their belts, which held all kinds of goodies—pepper spray, weapon-sized Swiss Army knives, tasers, and stakes, all of which I kept for myself. I was now a one-woman arsenal. Oh yeah, these guys knew they weren't just guarding any old facility. I guessed I was lucky they'd mistaken me for a turkey vulture. *Offended*, of course, but lucky. Otherwise they might have come with crossbows locked and loaded with wooden bolts. Or guns filled with holy water. Because nothing said horror like facing down a neon pink water pistol.

Then I frisked them.

"Hey, at least buy a guy dinner first," Pyro protested.

"A little to the right," his friend quipped, when I had my paws in *his* pockets.

"Okay, first off, *ewww*. And second … no, just ewww. And maybe *hell no*." I drew back with keycards and keys. "Why don't you use this time to think up some better lines? You may also consider how to update your résumés, because I'm pretty sure by tomorrow your positions will be available. Ta!"

I rose and looked around for any further surprises. I had, like, maybe a little over an hour left before dawn. Enough time to get in, get a glimpse, and get home? I had to hope so. The keycards would help as long as they didn't have any biometric sorts of scanners, like eyeball or fingerprint identification. I looked at the twits for a moment, trying to imagine cutting off fingers or popping out eyes to defeat the scanners, and just couldn't. Sure, I'd beat them up in the heat of battle, but actually maiming them … permanently … Something rose in my throat, scalding hot, actually burning its way up like lava or venom or …

I threw up in the bushes. It wasn't about them. It was about Kelly Swinter, if that was her I'd left behind in the fire. And me. And how far I'd go. You didn't fight a war without casualties, right? But if this was a war, whose side was I on?

I wiped my mouth and straightened, seeing two sets of eyes on me in the night. Like they *knew*. I couldn't do the eyes. I just couldn't. But the finger … Could I?

"Tell me now," I said, looking over them. "What kind of security am I facing inside? Retinal scans?" I'd remembered the word for eyeball access. "Facial recognition? What?"

They exchanged looks, and I knew they were silently trying to coordinate their stories. Whatever came out would be lies.

"Nothin' like that," Pyro lied. "Keycards, video cameras, more guards like us."

I saw his partner roll onto his hands just slightly, as if out of sight would keep them out of mind, and I had my real answer.

I grabbed up the flashlight that had already seen so much action and knocked them both out. I couldn't have them calling for help once I'd gone, and it would be so much easier to do what I had to do if they weren't awake to feel the pain or watch me. I chose Pyro, and tried to take just the pads of his fingers—thumb and index. His Bic-flicking fingers. I almost tossed my cookies again as I cut into him with his own Swiss Army knife. I tried to focus on *my* friends and the idea of one of them in a facility like this ... Marcy or my spy-sister Cassandra; Trevor or Di or any of the others I'd gotten into this whole spy game, all unwittingly. Even Alistaire, psycho-psychic, who was soooo not my problem, didn't deserve to do time as a lab rat. Still, I hated myself just a little. But I hated the thought of failure more.

The portion of the facility farthest away from me was burnt out and boarded up. Rubble, a dumpster, and a cement truck sat silently down at that end. On my end the windows were still boarded, but there was no rubble. Not only did it seem untouched by fire, but access had been upgraded with a keycard reader and, sure enough, fingerprint scanner. At least my butchery wasn't in vain.

Totally grossed out as I did it, I pressed Pyro's prints into the plate, swiped his card, and stepped aside as the door whooshed open, just in case any surprises awaited me. Artificially cool air came spilling out, but nothing else. No additional guards. I stepped inside and let the door close behind me. It looked like this used to be the emergency area of the clinic. The doors opened right onto a waiting room with natty chairs and a window in one wall where a receptionist would control any further access inside. Only there was no receptionist. There *were* two vacant chairs where Tweedle-Dumb and Tweedle-Dumber outside had probably sat watching the various security bells and whistles, but I had the lobby all to myself.

There was another keycard scanner beside the receptionist/security window, but I listened at the door before using it. No sounds escaped. Either the coast was clear or the place was soundproofed. I was going to have to find out sooner or later, and I was burning night. I swiped the card, opened the door, and slipped through, closing it behind me—only to be faced with a currently unmanned nurses' station. A blinking red light went ignored. A hallway spun off from the station in both directions, all covered in bathroom-white tile and smelling of bleach so strong it singed my nose hairs. Not that I was using them for anything.

This is too easy. The thought kept playing over and over again in my head. I mean, I was good, but these were the *Feds.* They were supposed to be better. I crept to the first door on the right and peeked inside the postage-flap-sized window, crisscrossed with metal reinforcements that resembled chicken wire. My breath caught. Inside, bound to a bed, was someone who looked more skeleton than man ... his skin nearly collapsed in on his bones as if all the muscle supporting the flesh had melted away. His eyes were closed, but twitched as though he were dreaming ... nightmares, most likely. An IV pole stood on one side of his bed, the unmistakable red of blood dripping down through the tubes into his sunken wrist. On the other side stood a cart, another red-filled tube extending to it from his other arm. At first I couldn't understand why. Blood in, blood out. Pointless much?

Then a horrible, horrible thought occurred to me.

What if ... could anyone really be so bloody-minded? *What if,* the voice inside my head pressed, relentless, the Feds were using this guy and maybe others as, like, super-serum generators? Was that even possible? I mean, I had an idea of what our vampire blood could do. On my last mission, I'd brought a guy back from a coma with only a few drops. Could they be using vamps as living miracle cures—milking them like dairy cows? On the one hand, I couldn't quite blame them. Our blood could do a lot of good. But could any end justify this means—creating a living skeleton, if you could even call it living? Given their methods, how noble could their motives be? I somehow doubted our blood would be made available to the needy, like those at the top of transplant lists. More likely it would be reserved for the elite, the power brokers, or those who could pay to finance that power.

For all I knew, it had other side effects too, beyond super healing. I hadn't waited around long enough to see what lasting effect my blood might have had on my newfound friend Bram, aka coma boy. He might have developed fashion sense or super speed or the ability to blow acid snot-bubbles... Would the Feds come up with a way to create super-soldiers or spies who didn't have our sunlight limitations? If so, what would become of us? Fodder to generate their serum?

Maybe I was getting ahead of myself. I didn't have any evidence that this vampire wasn't some brain-dead specimen the Feds were merely taking advantage of... not that it sounded much better when I thought of it that way. I had to know more.

I moved to the next door, but before I could see inside, an alarm went off. Something must have given me away! Blue lights started to strobe inside the halls, bouncing brightly off the gleaming white tile. The sound was enough to shatter eardrums, especially those as sensitive as mine. I clapped my hands over my ears and bolted back the way I'd come. But the sirens had drowned out the sounds of running feet—there were security guys and a security gal headed my way.

I tried my keycard on the closest door, but got a red light.

Denied. Capture was just a millisecond away. The hall I was in dead-ended a few doors down. I was trapped. I looked left and right for some miracle or inspiration and finally thought to look up.

"Hold it right there!" a voice ordered. But there was no way in hell that was happening.

The ceiling was made of those foamlike squares, also white, held in place by a lattice of metal slats. I could bust through it easily. The trick would be finding something up there to support my weight. But I didn't have a choice. I bent at the knees and prepared to launch myself into the air. Security drew on me; it was now or never. I leapt. A bullet blew its way through my knee, shattering my sanity with the pain and whiting out my vision, but I was already airborne.

I hit a pipe in the ceiling and instinctively grabbed on for all I was worth. One leg wouldn't work, but I swung the other up over the pipe and used it to push me forward like an inchworm on speed. Even with my war wound I was supernaturally fast.

More shots were fired ... one grazed my ear and I cursed, hoping it hadn't hit my piercing. I'd heal, but the lobe would come back whole and unpierceable. If the spy game cut down on my body beautification options, someone was going to die. Another bullet hit me in the thigh of the leg I was already dragging, but I didn't let that stop me. I scrambled along my pipe until I couldn't anymore, either physically or logistically. Too much else was in the way. But I'd outrun the gunshots for now, and I'd gone far enough to put a few rooms between me and the guards. I had to get down and figure out an escape route.

I dropped my good leg down through one of the ceiling tiles and the rest of my body fell with it. I landed badly in a room with a crash cart and IV but no body, the outside windows boarded up like all the rest. In the hallway, I heard yelling, running, doors being flung back … a room-to-room search.

Quick as thought, I grabbed the IV pole and swung it at the boarded-up window. It shattered, but the glass was held in by the thick boards on the outside. I swung again as the door opened behind me. The board exploded outward, and my shoulder exploded in pain at the same time, but I dove through the window and was off at hyper-human speed, ignoring my body's need to crumple each time I came down on my bad leg. I could sense the pursuit behind me, but if security got off any other shots, they never struck home. I was up and over the fence, running for my life before they could get a bead on me.

Truth be told, I don't remember much of the mad dash to Hunter's car. I was leaping the fence and the next thing I knew, I was bleeding all over his seats. Time and torment were playing tricks on me. I yelled at him to "Drive, drive, DRIVE!" He was already peeling out before I finished. I guessed my gunshot wounds had given away the urgency.

"You need a hospital?" he asked.

"Why? You're a doctor."

"I'm a *dentist*."

"Whatever. Anyway, there's no time. Just get me home."

I could feel the bullet in my thigh working itself out, hurting like hell as it did. I clamped down on a scream. Fresh blood would make the healing go a lot faster, but I didn't drain and drive. I'd died once by car already; I wanted to mix it up. If I went down again, it was going to be in a blaze of glory.

I dug furrows into Hunter's leather seats with my nails, clenching against the pain, but by the time we'd reached my place and the sky had begun to pinken the faintest bit, the worst was over. I was as weak as a kitten, but healed enough that I'd probably survive. It was the least of my worries, though. I'd come up with that clever exit strategy of switching places with Mina, but I hadn't really gotten as far as re-entry.

"How far are you willing to go with this?" I asked Hunter.

"What do you mean?" Hunter slid his attention from the road to me.

"Are you willing to sacrifice your car—risk some body work, anyway? I need to get back into my apartment unseen. I need a distraction."

"A car accident?"

"Yup. Your car, their rear end."

"But my insurance—"

"I don't think it'll come to that," I answered, rolling my eyes. *Big picture here, dude.*

He thought for a second, then I could actually see his shoulders square and his jaw tighten. "I'm in."

"Good. Let me out around the corner, give me a second to get into place, and then come flying around that corner like a bat outta hell."

He nodded.

"And give me your cell phone. I need to let Mina know to be at the front door when she hears that crash."

That way, the door would only have to open once. I could dash in and she could slip out at the very moment of impact and no one would be the wiser.

Except for Hunter and his smashed Subaru.

12

As usual, day knocked me out, and I slept the sleep of, well, the dead. No counting sheep, no dreams. Just here, then gone, then suddenly here again with the setting of the sun.

I woke to the sound of my phone ringing—one of them, anyway. It was muffled, and if not for my vampire senses, I might not have heard it at all.

Groaning, I got out of bed. All my limbs were back in working order, but it took my brain a little longer to come online. I had a moment of confusion when I couldn't find the phone before I realized I'd stowed it away in a drawer the night before, when I'd slipped out. By the time I got to it, I'd missed the call, but seeing that it was Agent Stick-up-her-butt—er, Maya—I called back instantly.

"Hey, I just missed—"

"Where were you last night?" she cut in sharply.

I blinked. "Well, hello to you too."

"I asked you a question."

This was one of those moments where if my heart could beat, it would be pounding like that of an adrenaline junkie or caffeine freak or stylista during fashion week. It should never even have occurred to her that I hadn't been home all night.

"Right here," I answered. "You know that. You've got surveillance on me, for goodness sake. You've probably got me Lojacked."

"You didn't answer your phone."

"When?"

"*Last night*," she bit out.

"You must have called while I was in the shower. Crappy cell service in there, if you must know. I blame the ceramic tile."

"And afterward?"

"Afterward, what?"

"*Messages.*" I could practically see the steam coming out of her ears from here.

"I didn't check. Sorry! Why, what happened?" I'd practiced the innocent voice on my parents, so I knew I could pull it off. Sadly, she wasn't getting the full glare of the innocent *look*, which really sold it.

"One of our facilities was broken into last night."

"And you think it was me?" I asked, playing up shock.

"The description matched."

"Petite, stylish, irresistible?"

She choked, and, if I didn't know better, I'd have thought it was a repressed laugh. Well, the repressed part fit, anyway. "Female vampire, dark hair, small stature, heart-shaped face ... sound like anyone we know?"

Well, crap. "Half the models in *Teen Vogue*," I quipped. "But then, I guess we can't count them among us vamps, since they photograph so well. Let me think—"

"Don't bother. You're needed at the Tower tonight."

"I don't know that it's such a good idea for me to show up there empty-handed. The vamps made it very clear the cost of doing business with them ... I need to bring in Nelson Ricci—Dion. It's the only way to prove myself."

"That's exactly why we need you there. Brent and Marcy have turned up a new lead, someone who apparently escaped Dion's cult. If they question him themselves, they blow their cover, but if they give you the nod—"

"I can get him alone and convince him to spill his guts. Got it. But what if he's a trap. I mean, cults aren't exactly known for being easy to leave."

"You'll have backup."

"Brent and Marcy?" Wouldn't running to my rescue blow their cover just as surely as doing the interview themselves?

"Bobby. He'll meet you there."

"But—"

"Relax. The vamps had you in that wine bar, didn't they? Selene, anyway. If they'd been desperate to have Bobby, they could have pulled him in right then. There's something else that they want more. Or, at least, first."

"Nelson."

"Bingo."

That led right into the question I'd been dreading but could no longer fail to ask. "Back at the Radner fire..." My heart ached even if it couldn't beat. "You didn't find any of Nelson's, uh, people, did you? Any bodies, I mean?"

Maya was silent for a second, then asked, "Who should we have found?"

The air I took in to get the words out felt like hot tar and stuck in my chest.

"No one," I answered, forcing the words out. "I just wondered. In the thick of battle—" *I thought I killed someone,* I didn't finish, not out loud.

"*No one?*" she repeated, clearly disbelieving. "Well, if they had a man down, they took him away with them."

Crap, that was an idea that had never even occurred to me. It had taken me almost twenty-four hours to work up the courage to even ask, and I'd been too busy sneaking around to check out the news. I'd almost been prepared to live with fear and uncertainty about what had happened rather than risk the sure knowledge of what I'd done. But now that I'd faced my fears... I *still* didn't know about Kelly Swinter. It didn't seem likely that Nelson and his brood would have gone to the trouble of taking a body with them, though. They didn't strike me as the sentimental types. So either she was alive or they had some sinister purpose in taking the corpse... Somehow, I didn't find myself entirely comforted.

To outrun my thoughts, I turned, as always, to fashion. The Feds had supplied me with a few fashion faux pas along the pseudo-vampire line, including a shiny black vinyl dress and matching knee-high boots with a wedge heel that would give me at least another four inches in height that I sorely needed. Give me a whip and a funky mask and I could practically be Catwoman. Never in a million years would I have chosen the outfit for myself, but tonight that was kinda the point. I didn't want to be me. I wanted to be Cosette D'Ampir, ubervamp, or Gayle Kuttner, super spy, or … anyone else. Wearing vinyl seemed like a kind of penance.

It was time to go clubbing with the fanged and fabulous.

• • •

I wouldn't say that the Tower was packed, but even midweek it drew a pretty good crowd. They weren't all as wildly dressed as on the night of the vampire ball, but I wasn't the only one in vinyl. In fact, there was enough vinyl around that I wondered how many old records had died for our fashion sins. I'd left my hair free-flowing tonight, and it hung in waves down to my butt, nearly as black as my dress. If it weren't for the wide red belt I'd found and my fire-engine-red lipstick, you'd have sworn I was drawn in black-and-white, given my pallor.

Even though the spy game was all about blending in, I turned at least one head. The guy checking IDs at the door—no cover charge tonight—looked more punk than goth. His fauxhawk was tortured into a hard ridge on top of his head, like the back sail on some prehistoric lizard, and his head alone probably held enough hardware to set off metal detectors just driving past the airport—brow, lip, nose, and when he spoke I noticed it was tongue, too. Not the ears, though. Those had the big wooden plugs in lieu of earrings. It was a hardcore look, but I didn't think it'd be all that when he was tripping over his earlobes in a few years.

"You alone?" he asked, looking me up one side and down the other, which was pretty pointless since I was totally symmetrical.

"Not for long," I answered, wondering how long it would take Selene or Very Scary to catch me. Oh, I could have called ahead, but that would have taken all the fun out of things.

"I'm on break in twenty minutes. I could buy you a drink," he said, missing the point.

"I'm spoken for. Thanks anyway." I moved on inside.

He shrugged like it didn't matter and turned back to the door, half-thrashing my ego. It was official—if I ever started my own entourage, he was right out.

No Bobby, no Marcy or Brent on the first floor, so I climbed to the second. That's where most of the action was, and certainly the volume. Techno music poured out of every speaker. It wasn't jam-packed this time—which was good for the caped crusader thrash-dancing by himself at the edge of the dance floor—but there were enough people to fill the room. I was halfway across it before I spotted Brent grinding up against the aviatrix of the Burgess Brigade. Her goggles were up on top of her fiery red hair, holding it back like a headband. Her fawn-colored leggings were skintight, like riding pants, and her white men's shirt was unbuttoned to where I could see her bra peeking out—black, like her boots. I didn't think she was very authentic, but what did I know. I bet Marcy was grinding her teeth down to itty-bitty nubs. Luckily, they'd grow back.

Brent caught my eye and nodded deeper into the club, to where the rest of the Brigade stood holding up the back wall. I hoped the bump-and-grind was mission related … for Marcy's sake.

Speaking of whom … I found her there, among a gaggle of admirers, shooting poisonous glances at the dance floor. I got caught up in one, but her face changed immediately at the sight of me and she was able to turn the resulting smile onto one of her suitors. You'd never know it wasn't still dress-up night at the sight of them: the maharajah; a guy who looked like Johnny Depp as the Mad Hatter; and the clockwork gentleman who'd caught my eye outside the club that first night. He was another Johnny Depp look-alike, but a much hotter version, like maybe from *Sleepy Hollow*. Bad movie, smokin' hero.

Apparently there hadn't been time yet to create Marcy's doomsday dress, because she sat among them in widow's weeds—a small hat with a black veil (the real thing, not the vampire Magna Carta) and a dark lace gown with a collar that rose high around the back and scooped daringly low in the front to reveal scads of cleavage. A silver-wrapped vial dangled between her breasts, drawing the eye to the assets that were pushed and smooshed to attention. On her right hand, she wore a poison ring. I wondered if it was loaded and, if so, whether Brent or his dancing girl were entirely safe. Marcy twirled a dark curl absently around and around her ring finger as if considering the question herself.

The maharajah was holding forth, and stopped suddenly as he realized he'd lost everyone. He turned a cranky face toward me, which changed quickly as he took in my vinyl dress and four-inch heels. Marcy's other two admirers looked me over as well.

"You're the girl who got pulled into the inner sanctum the other night," the hotter Johnny Depp said.

I gave him one of my coyest smiles. "I am. And you are?"

"Guy Fawkes," he said with a bow. "And my companions are Ghedri, Terrence"—the maharajah and hatter bowed in turn—"and the fair Raven." He used the introduction as an excuse to take and kiss Marcy's hand, probably trying to one-up her other suitors.

"Pleased to make your acquaintance," I responded. I refused to curtsey in this dress. I wasn't sure the seams could handle it.

"Your name, dear lady?" Guy Fawkes prompted.

"Oh, sorry. I'm Cosette. Of course, I noticed you all the other night and was hoping that I might have the chance to speak with you."

"Just speak?" he asked, giving me a "come hither" sort of look. I bet in good light it worked like a charm.

"For now," I flirted back.

Marcy used their distraction as a chance to shoot another poisoned glance at the dance floor, twisting her curl nearly to the breaking point.

"Raven, is it?" I asked, calling Marcy's attention back to me. "I have a particular fascination with poison rings." *Well, rings in general.* "I was wondering about yours. Is it a working model?"

Marcy yanked her gaze back to the group and took her cue just as expected.

"Absolutely. An antique as well. Would you care to see it?"

"I'd love to, but perhaps we should step over into better light. Boys, if you would excuse us?"

Marcy touched each of their arms as she stood and passed by, promising to return shortly. I thought I heard one of them mutter something about every moment of her absence being an eternity, but no one could be that sappy. Right?

"I'm going to kill him," Marcy said as we moved out of earshot, which didn't take more than a few steps given the pounding music. We stopped in a decently lit spot near the dance floor.

"Brent?" I asked.

"Ye-ah," she said. "I'm not going to kill just anyone."

I pretended that made sense … and that I was utterly fascinated with her poison ring.

"He's not that into her," I said with a shrug.

"How can you tell?"

"I thought you weren't interested in Brent?"

"Gina!"

"Okay, okay. I can tell because his eyes were scanning the room and not her. He saw me as soon as I got upstairs."

"Really?"

Oh yeah, she was totally indifferent. "I swear," I said.

"Thanks. You're the best." She took the ring off and handed it to me to try on, showing me first how to release the hidden catch.

"I know it. Have you seen Bobby?"

"Not yet."

"What about the guy I'm supposed to grill?"

"It's Terrence."

"The guy who looks like the Mad Hatter?"

"I know, right?"

"Got it." I handed her the ring back and we returned

to the men, chatting away about poisons. She was, anyway. The Feds must have briefed her for her role. Must have, because she couldn't really be that into death, could she? A BFF would know.

I debated waiting for Bobby, but for all I knew he was watching from afar. Plus, I suspected I'd do better with the Mad Hatter on my own than with an escort.

"I'm off to the bar," I announced when we got back to the group. "Anyone else want anything?"

"Terrence, love, would you get me a bloody Mary?" Marcy asked. "I think I need some electrolytes or something. I'm feeling a little—" She swayed dramatically on her feet. Ghedri and Guy rushed to help her.

"Anything for m'lady," Terrence said hurriedly, not even questioning why *I* couldn't fetch and carry. Oh, she was good.

I took Terrence's arm and held it in an iron grip as I steered him away from the clan. When I had him all to myself, I leaned in close. "So, I hear you were in with Dion's group. What's it like inside the cult?"

He jumped, and instantly tried to get his arm back, but I wasn't going to let him get away that easily. "I—I don't want to talk about that."

"Too bad," I said heartlessly. I let an ominous note creep into my voice. "You heard them say I was pulled into the club's inner sanctum. You don't think I was called in for nothing, do you?" I didn't know what they all thought went on in there, but clearly the inner sanctum was a source of awe. I could use that.

"What do you mean?" There was a tremor in his voice. I didn't want to be proud of putting it there, but…

I licked my lips, slowly, and that was clearly all he could take. There must have been fang showing. Really convincing fang. I ran my tongue over my teeth to check, lingering on the canines. Yup, sure enough.

"Nevermind. I'll tell you whatever you want to know, okay? Your boy Dion ... he's lost it."

"Lost it how? What did you see?"

"I don't"—he swallowed—"I don't want to talk about that."

"Terrence, we've been over this. You're not going anywhere until you tell me."

His gaze darted left and right, as if looking for rescue. He pulled away again, testing that there was still no escape, which, of course, there wasn't.

"The girl," he said finally. "They fell on her like dogs. And now, the way they have her hooked up like some kind of Frankenstein's lab experiment ... "

"You said *they*, but you were a part of it. Weren't you?"

I could see the whites all around his eyes. He didn't answer right away, which was answer enough.

"I got out," he said defensively.

"And they just let you go?"

His gaze stopped rolling around the room and he looked at me, really looked at me for a moment ... and then his attention caught on something over my shoulder.

"Focus, Terrence. Come back to me. Who are *they*? What girl? I need you to tell me about her." Who could it be? Elise's former roommate, Kinesha Williams? Someone we didn't know about?

But the sanity train had left the station. "No," he said

in a hush, as if to himself. "No, they didn't. They couldn't. They're here."

He yanked at his arm, like his life depended on getting it free, like he'd leave it behind with me if he could just so the rest of him could escape. I looked over my shoulder to see who he was so afraid of, and froze.

Kelly Swinter sat at the bar, drinking something froufrou and pink. She raised it when she saw me glancing her way. She looked a little rough around the edges, which made sense for someone who'd only the night before been drained nearly to death and left behind in a burning building. But she also looked dark, deadly, determined, and completely fixated on us.

"Come on," I said, tugging on the arm Terrence was so desperate to free.

"Where are we going?" he asked.

"Out of here, that's for sure."

"Oh, thank God. I didn't think they'd dare come back, but—"

"Less talk, more walk."

Terrence nearly lost his footing on the stairs, but a hand came out of nowhere to grab him and keep him from falling on his face. And attached to the hand was a nice arm... *very* nice, as I knew from intimate experience.

"Our informant?" Bobby asked, his gaze meeting mine and zapping me with that current that always threatened to restart my heart. Took my breath away every time.

"Our informant," I agreed. "We're getting him out of here."

"Then let's go." Bobby cleared the way down the stairs,

but as we got to the ground floor, I saw Elise lurking by the entrance.

"This way." I aimed us all for the side door leading into the alley where Hunter had caught up with me the first night.

The door was propped open, as I'd known it would be, for people coming out for smokes. I yanked it wider and burst through, Terrence huffing and puffing at my side, Bobby one step behind me.

All of us headed right into a trap.

13

The door slammed shut behind us. I only had time to take in the sight of Nelson, Elise, and some new muscle-headed minion before I was whirling to face whatever was coming from behind. *Kelly*, still looking as pale as the grave, launched herself away from the alley door, swinging some kind of flat wooden bat with nails driven through it straight for my head. Bobby threw Terrence to the side, out of the way of the fight, and jumped in front of the bat, catching the impact with his outstretched hand. One of the nails pierced right through it, the blood lashing my eye, which I closed just in time.

Then one of those I'd turned my back on brought a

second bat crashing down on my head, and my world shattered into sharp shards of pain. I went down to my knees.

Behind me, Bobby gave an animalistic cry and suddenly Kelly went flying through the air toward my attacker. I didn't know whether he'd flung her off her bat or picked her up with his mental mojo—telekinesis was a wonderful thing—but either way, it was effective. Kelly struck Elise and both hit the pavement hard. Unfortunately, Nelson and his muscle-headed Burly Boy were still standing and rushed in to take the girls' place.

"Stop!" Bobby ordered, reaching for his other power, telepathy. He could compel others as well as talk mind-to-mind.

Burly Boy halted, but Nelson didn't so much as flinch. Of course he'd be one of the few who, like me, was immune to the compulsion.

Seeing him still rushing at Bobby, I rallied and got to my feet, swaying from the pain in my head that threatened to split me down the middle. Terrence, I noticed, was trying to crawl away, but one of the downed girls who'd landed nearby reached out to grab his ankle in a death grip. He cried out, but Bobby was my bigger concern. The world stopped moving on me just in time to see Bobby dodge the bat Nelson swung at him and then yank it out of his hand. He never saw the threat in the other hand coming—Nelson pulled a stake from a waistband or pocket or thin air and before I could react, it was buried in Bobby's chest.

He went down hard, and my heart went with him. The seams of my dress ripped as I let out a mighty roar and scissor-kicked Nelson, catching him right under the chin as he spun away from Bobby's fountaining blood. I didn't spare a glance for where he fell, but dropped to Bobby's side immediately, afraid to touch him, more afraid not to.

His eyes were open and he was staring at me, his mouth opening, but nothing coming out. The stake had hit right of center. Or maybe that was just my wishful thinking. The heart was slightly *left*, right? No, the stake couldn't have hit his heart. I insisted. Not Bobby. He wasn't going anywhere. He was *mine*.

I dragged a nail across my wrist and got some drops into his open mouth before hands clenched on my shoulders and dragged me away. Burly Boy, free from Bobby's compulsion, had caught me. I fought against him like a wildcat, needing to get back to Bobby, to see if he'd swallowed, if he was alive. I didn't know ... they never covered this kind of thing in super-spy training. Should I have pulled the stake? Could he heal with it still stuck inside him?

"Bobby!" I cried out, like that would help, like his name alone would bring him back from the dead.

"Take her," Nelson ordered. "And Terrence."

"What about *him*?" Burly Boy asked, nodding at Bobby.

"He's no good to anyone anymore."

"Nooo!" I didn't know if I said it out loud. I didn't know anything anymore except that *he could NOT die*. Not for real. I kicked out again and managed to catch Burly Boy in the shin. He cried out and dropped all his weight onto his other leg, momentarily unbalanced so that when I hurled myself to the side, he had to let me go or fall along with me.

The girls were up again. Elise held Terrence in an

inescapable grip, but Kelly was free and, like her two friends, fully focused on me. It was three against one.

A war cry sounded from the end of the alley, drawing all eyes before the killer kids could jump me again.

Eric appeared out of nowhere, looking like something out of one of the *Librarian* movies. The crazy inventor came charging at us, swinging a cane from which he pulled a slender sword.

The kids didn't wait for us to bring the fight to them. Burly Boy dove for me again, sheer fists of fury since he'd lost his bat. I was unarmed but ready for him this time, and sidestepped, grabbing his arm as he went by to propel him forward—face-first, I hoped, into the pavement.

Eric reached my side, waving the sword around wildly to ward off the others and pulling something that looked like a watch out of his pocket. This was so not the moment to check the time. I was pretty sure the killer kids agreed. I could tell by their body language that Nelson and Kelly were getting ready to spring when a blur of motion came from behind and Eric dropped like a ton of bricks. Burly Boy had found his bat and used it upside Eric's head. I was next. Too stunned by everything that had just happened to dodge this blow, I went down, Eric's body half-breaking my fall.

"You'd better not have scrambled his brains," Nelson growled at Burly Boy. "We need him."

"His powers, not his mind," Burly protested, crossing his arms over his chest.

"Just pray they're not one and the same. Load him up with the others," he ordered.

I was grabbed roughly and tossed over Burly Boy's

shoulder like a sack of potatoes. The metal baseboards of the van cracked my back, but it was my front getting all the attention as Burly Boy felt me up, searching for contraband. He found my two phones and tossed them into the alley just as Nelson threw Eric in next to me. Elise thrust Terrence in as well. The latter scuttled to a corner of the van, where he huddled in a protective ball.

My heart ached for Bobby as the doors slammed shut, locking us in and him out. I couldn't help seeing that stake in his chest, blood pouring out, the vacant look on his face...I called out to him mentally to *fight*, to live. Though I knew they couldn't hear me, I even cried out silently to Marcy and Brent to find him and to the universe at large. Bobby had a destiny. The psycho-psychic had said so. He hadn't yet achieved it, and therefore... *He. Could. Not. Die.*

No one answered me. No one.

The whole van smelled like blood—Eric's, mine, Burly Boy's. Strangely, not Nelson's. If anyone had gotten in a decent blow at him, it hadn't so much as broken the skin. I wished him internal bleeding and much of it.

I needed to get some of that blood into me, to build up my strength so we could escape and take the kids down. Because I *would* take them down for what they did to Bobby. If it was the last thing I ever did.

I tested my strength. Sure enough, my legs twitched when I told them to and the rest of my body was coming back online, recovering from the repeated blows to the head that had knocked me all but senseless. Another minute or two and I could probably wrestle a kitten into submission. Maybe even a full-grown cat.

Nelson was too smart to get close enough for me to grab. But Eric...surely he wouldn't mind donating some blood to aid his escape. Maybe I could just lap up some of the blood that was free-flowing from his head wound, clean it up a little for him. But after what had happened with Kelly, I was still a little afraid to feed in need. What if I lost myself again and couldn't stop in time? Eric I actually liked.

I inched toward him, hoping the motion of the van would mask my movement. I'd no sooner gotten close than Nelson grabbed me by my shiny red belt and yanked me against him instead, wrapping his arms around me to hold them to my sides, careful to keep all of his extremities outside biting range. I kicked and fought like an alley cat, but it didn't do me a bit of good. For someone who was human, he was preternaturally strong, and for someone who looked all of seventeen, he was supernaturally scary.

I craned my neck until I could look him in the eyes. If they were windows into the soul, his was a neglected locker room—ripe and rank with the stench of body odor, sweat socks, and dirty jock straps. In a word, vile.

"Who *are you*?" I gasped.

"I am *Chaos*."

"Go to hell, that's my title." Even if I didn't have the tiara and sash to prove it.

"The hell it is," he answered as the van careened wildly around a corner, sandwiching me between Eric's unconscious body and his own evil incarnate. My skin literally tried to crawl away from Nelson's touch, but there was no escaping the iron grip. I started to focus on survival, watching the windows, trying to see where we were so that when we got away...

We stopped after ten to twenty minutes of hell, and Burly Boy leapt out to raise a door by hand. I could hear it rattle along its groove, even though I couldn't really see from my position on the floor. Some sort of garage or loading bay door, from the sound of it. Either not automated or without power. A fat lot of good that knowledge did when a third of the state seemed to be for sale or foreclosure. Deserted sites were probably a dime a dozen. I needed more intel.

Nelson hauled me out roughly. "I've got this one."

Elise and Burly Boy reached for the others, and I saw Eric's eyelids flicker upward for a second. But if the light was on, no one was home. I didn't see any awareness, any fight. He was either a very good actor or Burly had really scrambled his brains with that blow to the head.

Nelson carried me through the hangerlike loading bay and into an area that looked like it used to be office space. The only things left behind were cheap metal carts, like the kind used to wheel supplies or mail around an office. Nelson started to tip me onto one of them as Burly Boy came through the door carrying Eric. The survival instinct rose up in me, and I kicked a foot free to send my cart careening into the next so that it slammed against the wall. Burly Boy dropped Eric to the floor to help Nelson with me. I clawed and kicked, but between them both they managed to get me up onto a cart and tied down with some kind of super-strong cord.

But I'd finally bloodied Nelson. He'd carry the scratches from my nails for a good long time. Maybe they'd even scar. A start on my payback for Bobby.

14

I lost myself for a little while, strapped down to an autopsy table while Burly Boy went back and forth poking me with needles and hooking me up to all kinds of things from a third cart they wheeled in. It looked like a mobile Frankenstein's lab, with bags, tubing, tools, and—most chillingly—a machine about the size of an old-school hatbox, like the one I'd kept all my curlers and scrunchies in back home. Eric's energy transference device? I looked over to see him strapped to the table beside me, his nutty-professor hair going every which way. He was awake and alert again, taking it all in with a mix of horror and fascination on his face.

"We're screwed," he said when Burly Boy left, apparently for the final time.

I couldn't help but agree. It wasn't like me to wallow. But *Bobby*...those wicked blue eyes dancing with mischief as he'd whipped my towel off back at headquarters, the way his lips tasted, the scent of him all good enough to eat...

Gina. I could almost hear his voice in my head, calling my name.

Gina, I'm here. Marcy and Brent got to me in time.

My mind was playing tricks on me.

Bobby? I asked, afraid to hope. *Is that really you?*

Next time, pull out the stake.

I laughed, and Eric looked at me like I was nuts, but if crazy meant Bobby was still alive, I'd take it.

I love you, I said without thinking. *Don't you dare let there be a next time.*

I'd surprised him. Don't ask me how I knew, I just did. It was one of those mind-speak things.

I love you too, he said back. *Always.*

If my heart didn't restart then, it never would. I loved him. So much it was stupid. Enough to feel alive again and then some. We were getting out of this, and I was going to kick killer-kid booty for them scaring me like that.

Where are you? he asked. He was getting fainter, fading away. This had to be a lot for him after everything he'd been through tonight.

Don't know. I tried to mentally send him everything I had, from the loading doors to the layout, but it wasn't much. No street names, nothing.

We'll find you, he promised.

I wasn't going to count on it, but at this point, just

knowing that Bobby was okay was enough. I could save myself. Hell, I could save us all. Maybe. Probably. I hoped.

I turned to Eric. "We're getting out of this."

"It's all my fault," he answered, even though I couldn't see what one thing had to do with the other.

"Huh?"

"I never thought about how the technology could be used. I developed it to give the wounded enough strength to hang on until they could get help or reach the top of a transplant list. Not … *this*." He nodded, and my gaze followed his to the hatbox-sized gizmo, the one they had me hooked to.

"What are they doing to me?"

"At a guess, draining both your blood and your strength. That's my energy transference machine. But they've modified it somehow."

"So your machines really do work … " I started, before I could help myself.

"Well, *of course* they work." He was getting fired up at my very suggestion. "Why do you think Nelson's friends wanted them so badly? They came back for this machine at the pawnshop, didn't they? But I never considered they'd use it on *vampires*." He glared at me accusingly. "You and your people are like rechargeable batteries. You can keep going and going. Anyone in possession of my work can keep draining and draining, transferring your energy. If you live forever, they can too."

"So it's basically an eternity machine?!" I didn't mean it to come out quite so forcefully. I mean, Eric already felt responsible enough, but *damn* that was a lot to answer for.

"I didn't *know*."

I closed my eyes and tried to think. If Bobby and I were

right, it was Eric's power—his belief in a machine—that made it work. Upside: the killer kids couldn't possibly mass produce the gizmos without Eric's support. Downside: they didn't have to. If they wanted to live forever, grow up to rule the world, well, they were off to a strong start right now. And with no other Eric to go around, they had the market cornered on his technology. Plus, they now had him for handy blood donations to recharge the battery—aka *me*. Were Terrence and the girl he'd talked about being hooked up like a medical experiment in the same boat? Captive donors? Had Nelson, or whoever was walking around in his skin, figured out some way to have his cake and eat it too? Eternity *and* tanning options? And where was the real Nelson? Presumably with the fangs, trapped in the body of the vamp who'd stolen his.

"Where is Nelson now?" I asked.

"*Right here*," a voice answered. Right body, wrong brain.

Nasty-Nelson must have come in through a doorway out of my line of sight. "I came to check on my own personal fountain of youth," he added, appearing at the side of my autopsy table and picking up something from down to my left. I was no science geek, but I knew there was a name for the glass … thingy … he lifted to eye level. Bigger than a vial, smaller than a bread box. *Beaker*, that was it.

And in it … with all the fuss, I'd expected something flashy, I guess—shiny, like with little shooting stars or maybe bubbly like champagne—but the liquid in the beaker didn't even look like blood. They'd distilled it into something purer and more complex—blood plus drained-off energy, courtesy of Eric's invention, like some kind of super serum. It truly looked like nothing so much as water. Pure, filtered water, sure, with a hint of soap-bubble iridescence to it, but still … maybe it sparkled in the sun.

He held the glass to his nose and sniffed its contents like wine, closing his eyes to savor the scent. Then, without monologuing even for a second, he lifted the beaker, tilted his head back, and drank its contents down.

I gasped, and Nelson shuddered all over, his jaw dropping with the power of it. His hand spasmed open and the beaker fell to the floor, shattering into a million pieces, but he didn't even notice. And *that* was when the light show started. Tiny pinpricks of light, like dust motes caught by the sun, danced all along his flesh, giving him a glow like something out of a Biblical movie. For a second he looked like an angel fallen to earth, as pure and perfect and blissful as a man with a monobrow can manage. Then the effect faded, except that when he opened his eyes, the light was still there, shining through.

He turned that glowing gaze on Eric, who stared at him with shock.

"I never meant—" Eric started, then stopped as he seemed to decide that it didn't matter. I could almost watch him deflate as the fight seeped out of him … as he gave up.

"For it to be distilled?" Nelson finished for him. But Eric's eyelids did no more than flicker. "Well, you see, *uncle*, I've made a few tweaks to your design. All we needed was you— and then *poof*, you walked right into our hands. Your machine was so limited. Energy in, energy out. Both donor and donee had to be present. Sadly, not very practical. But if you distill the energy, mix in a little blood, and bottle it like a tonic, then you've got *control* and mobility. More than that, you have a miracle drug. The ultimate addiction. Extended life, health, vitality—all for a price."

"Don't call me that," Eric bit out, totally reacting to the wrong part of Nelson's whole horrifying speech.

"What—*uncle*? But you are, in a manner of speaking. Your little machines have a curious quirk ... they don't seem to work without you. But Nelson ... oh, he figured it out." It was totally eerie hearing Nelson talk about himself in the third person. "He was obsessed with my kind, you know. He wanted to prove useful, to cross over and live forever. That was why he brought us your first device. Why he brought us *you*."

"Then it's true. You've swapped bodies. He's still alive ... "

"Oh, I'm quite sure my friends are keeping my body, ah, warm for me, and him in it. But I really think that model is obsolete, don't you? So much more to experience in this body. The sun on my face. The joys of a steak dinner. *Garlic butter sauce*—oh, I'd almost forgotten the taste. So much more convenient to be an energy vampire, yes? As long as we have the bodies to drain. Lucky me, I know just the ones."

He kicked the glass shards from the beaker out of his way as he went for the door. "Keep up the good work," he added, turning back to us briefly. "I'll send in the others one by one as you recharge. In just a few hours, we should have everything we need to take on the others. All thanks to you, dear *uncle*."

Nelson disappeared, leaving behind silence except for Eric's repeated lifting of his head only to let it fall again to the table. But he didn't have enough height to dash his brains out, and I couldn't imagine he was doing better than giving himself ... and me ... a headache.

"Stop it!" I ordered. "We have to find a way out of this

before he gets what he needs." Because if I understood nasty-Nelson correctly, he wasn't just in this for himself. He planned to use my essence or whatever to bolster up a whole human army to go after the vamps. If he got control of the local vampires, he could make tons of his tonic. Enough for a private army or a thriving drug trade. Horror flooded me at the thought of the highest bidders. I could easily imagine entire armies of super soldiers, eternal dictators. And to sustain the vamps, feed the supply line, he'd need to kidnap more and more human donors.

Were Eric's inventions what the Feds had been after when they'd started their whole investigation? When the Swinter murders hit the fan, had they already been looking at Nelson as a way to get to Eric? Eric and his machines and their possibilities? His patent attempts and follow-up letters could easily have drawn down federal scrutiny. It was no wonder the Feds might want to nose around even the chance of a working mind-swap or energy transference machine. But did they want to stop, or control, the technology?

Bobby was way more the conspiracy theorist than me, but I didn't see any way that the government having the secrets to eternal life and strength would be a good thing. They might have a more focused agenda than the killer kids, so the serum probably wouldn't end up on the black market, but neither would it go to the underprivileged, like starving or abused kids. No, the drugs would be reserved for the high and mighty ... backroom deals, political dynasties. All battery powered. Oh hell no.

"We're both strapped to tables. What way out?" Eric asked hopelessly, cutting through my thoughts.

"I don't know. You're the genius. Figure it out. Think of your nephew. If you ever want to see him alive again and back in his real body, you'll come up with something."

I strained at my restraints, looking for some of that super-vamp strength I was supposed to have, but nasty-Nelson was draining it out of me as fast as the blood was resupplying. Or faster. Right now, Care Bears could probably wrestle me into submission. But Bobby was still alive. My brain was still working. That had to count for something.

It was still working ... or trying to ... when Kelly came in for her drought. She drank it down with a smirk, staring at me the whole time, challenging me to do something about it. She gave me a venti-sized pinch on her way out that would've left me with a respectable bruise if I weren't a vamp and beyond all that petty crap. Still, I would get even. Not so much for me as for her family. How on earth could someone murder their own family? Or leave their sister scarred and orphaned? How did any rational person decide they wanted into a club that demanded permanently cutting ties as part of the initiation? Not just permanently—*fatally*. As in, once you're in, you're implicated. Guilty. No one and nowhere to go back to. Terrence had tried.

It wasn't until Elise's visit for her dose of my distilled energy that I got an idea. She'd have kicked her own butt if she knew she'd given it to me. Unlike Kelly, Elise didn't give a damn about me. She didn't have eyes for anything but the beaker. She swirled the contents around for a second, watching it slosh, and then drank it down in one gulp. Her face transformed almost instantly, and her eyes widened with wonder as she caught the glow coming off her skin. "I don't freakin' believe it," she said in a hush.

That was all, but it was enough. I realized right then that it was all about belief. Just not hers. This was about Eric and the power he didn't even realize he wielded. If he controlled his machines strictly on will and faith, then if I could just shake that faith I ought to be able to cause a power outage, maybe long enough to recover from the draining and break my bonds.

The only problem was, I kind of hated to do it. Right now it seemed like belief was all Eric had. But if I could get us out of this and restore his nephew, I was sure we could call it even.

"Eric," I whispered loudly, injecting false excitement into my voice, "I think the machine is failing. I'm feeling stronger!"

His eyes fluttered open, but his stare lacked his earlier intensity. "It's just a second wind. It'll pass."

"No, look—" I did my best to flex those fingers and toes I could no longer feel. Miracle of miracles, they obeyed, if not with super-sonic speed. There might even have been a little give in the restraints. Was I losing mass? Already? I'd totally never been one of those girls who thought skeletal was sexy. I liked my curves, dammit. Oh, we were so getting out of here. Like *now*.

"I think—I think maybe Nelson's tweaks weakened your design," I said. "It's faltering."

And just like that, I thought I could feel the power dip. My energy flared, just for a second.

"You think so?" he asked.

"You tell me. Does anyone understand what you do? Is it that easy to manipulate your designs?"

I saw the light of hope flash in his eyes. "No. No one

understands. I mean, distilling isn't rocket science, but... well, it's just not built that way. How do you feel now?"

"Definitely getting stronger." Maybe it was just the power of suggestion, but I *felt* it. I curled my hands into fists and strained against the straps, but I wasn't there yet. I pulled until I imagined my very veins standing out against my skin, but when I failed to get free, Eric let his eyes close again.

"Give me another minute. I just need to gather my strength."

"Sure," he answered, not opening his eyes.

I was losing him. "How on earth did you get to be an inventor if one little setback sends you into retreat?"

His eyes popped open and he glared. "My nephew's been body-snatched. We've been captured by serial killers and strapped to gurneys. You're wasting away. Forgive me if I don't rally."

I glared back. "No, I won't forgive you. And neither will Nelson." He looked gobsmacked, but awake at least. Alert. *Pissed.*

A shadow fell over us, and we both shut up. It was Burly Boy this time. He grabbed up the beaker and held it to the light. "Is this all?" he asked over his shoulder.

"She must be waning. It's getting near dawn," the Nelson-impersonator said from the doorway. I shot a glance at Eric to make sure he'd heard. He was paying attention all right. He had that thinking look Bobby got sometimes, where I could practically parade past him in a string bikini and he'd never notice.

"Drink it and let's go," nasty-Nelson told Burly Boy. "We'll be strongest while the vamps are at their weakest."

Now? They were going *now?* Crap on a crispy, crumbly cracker. As soon as the sun rose, I'd be dead to the world. Unable to do anything to stop them. Except for the really old, powerful vamps, we'd *all* be dead to the world. Unless the other vamps had some way-skilled human minions who could fight off the killer kids, they'd be sleeping ducks. If I was guessing correctly, the mysterious Xander who Dion had worked for had either created the monster or *was* the monster. I didn't know if he'd done it with the help of the other vamps or not. Either way, clearly he'd gone rogue. And no matter what, I wasn't sure the vamps deserved what was coming to them, especially if their energy loss was to be the killer kids' gain.

I called out to Bobby as Burly Boy drank me in—and once again, for the record, *ewwww.* No answer. If I got out of this alive, I vowed, I'd have to see if Eric could build Bobby some kind of psychic voicemail. Or call waiting.

More desperately, I called, *Bobby!*

Here, he answered, as though from very far away. *Gina, are you okay?*

Quickly, I answered. I didn't know how much time there was until dawn, but it couldn't be much. I tried to keep my eyes open, but—*They're going after the vamps.*

Who? What?

The killer kids, I said with effort. *They're going to strike. Now.*

But—

My eyes shut with finality. My panic that Bobby was likewise fading, that I was too late to get the word out, receded along with the rest of the world.

15

ina! Come on, girl, wake up!" I was being shaken from side to side, a terrible metal clacking nearly splitting my head open.

"*Come on*," the voice insisted. "You said to rally, and I'm rallying."

Eric? But—

I forced my eyes open and turned my head to focus on an extreme close-up of the nutty professor. Somehow, he must have rocked his gurney across the room and into mine, because he was right freakin' there next to me, practically eyeball to eyeball.

"Night already?" I asked, knowing somehow that it wasn't. It didn't feel right, but then, how—?

"Day. I managed to get close enough to manipulate the machine. I'm feeding you *my* energy. Directly. No distillation. I hope it's enough."

I stared at him in awe. "You can do that?"

He demonstrated the limited movement he had with his hands in the straps. "Wasn't easy, and they've got a lead on us, but ... yeah. Are you strong enough now to bust out of here?"

"I'll have to be, won't I?"

I closed my eyes and summoned my inner diva. Show me a diva who can't bust her way out of a bad situation, and I'll show you a poser not worthy of the name. But my inner diva failed me. Nasty-Nelson certainly knew how to bind vamps. He'd been one himself. How could I fight an enemy who knew all my weaknesses and had left his own behind?

Okay, diva down. *Think, think, think.* Strength wasn't working. I'd have to come up with something else. I was fairly bird-boned. If it weren't for my curves, I might even be considered waifish. Already, I seemed to have lost mass. Maybe the trick was to think *small.* I contorted my hands until they were as tiny as I could make them, my fingers all pressing in on each other. I played to my weakness, thinking itsy, bitsy, insubstantial ...

Something was happening. I gave my hands a sharp tug, hoping to jolt them free from the restraints. My fingers were tingling again—my whole body, really, as if I were bathing in Pop Rocks. My eyes snapped open, and I nearly had a freak-attack. I was about to face plant into the ceiling tiles, and that made no sense at all!

I shrieked and dropped hard, falling back to my metal table and bruising my backside.

Eric was gaping at me. "Why didn't you just do that in the first place?"

I stared at him, his energy buzzing through me along with the adrenaline overload left over from my terror.

"Do what? What did I do?"

"You *misted*, went all ghostly. Just like in the old vampire tales. I didn't know you could do that."

"Neither did I." And neither did Nelson, if he'd left us here without taking any other precautions, so this couldn't be a common thing. Maybe it was due to a part of me being *Chaos* and doing the unexpected. If I ever found out where the Feds were keeping Alistaire, the psycho-psychic who'd named me that, I was going to demand answers. I imagined him strapped to his own gurney in some Federal facility and hoped his psychic ability told him I'd be coming to the rescue … someday. And then we would have a serious heart-to-heart. Although, asking Alistaire the right questions might give him way too much information. He wasn't the kind you trusted with your secrets. Or your sister. Or your cell phone, for that matter.

I could worry about all that later. For now, I had a hot new superpower! Even beyond my killer fashion sense, my vampire speed, strength, and all that. There was a tiny little part of me that feared this too was fueled by Eric's belief, but I squashed it like a bug. I was no machine, which was where his power lay.

Quickly, I got to work on Eric's restraints.

"Grab your machine," I ordered when I had him free and the blood donation thingie hooked up to him torn out. "And anything else that looks like a weapon or an indication of their plans." Yeah, because they were just going to leave things like that lying around. "I'm going to find a phone and some wheels."

I didn't trust the Feds but I needed them for now, at least as long as the faux vamps were the bigger threat. After that … I didn't know. I was a seat-of-the-pants kind of girl.

I dialed Maya's number from memory. She answered on the second ring with a terse, "Yes." Probably the phone I'd found came up *Restricted* or *Caller Unknown* on her ID.

"Maya, it's Gina. Listen quickly, because I've got to run. The killer kids are after the vamps. The ringleader, Nelson Ricci, is actually possessed by one of them." As I talked, the phone pressed between my ear and shoulder, I tossed the lair-like room next to the one where Eric and I had been held. The phone had been in one of the drawers of a huge but worse-for-wear entertainment center taking up one wall. I'd also found tasers, a gross of those blasted zip-tie cuffs, piles of pizza boxes, some illegal substances, and dirty clothes strewn every which way, but no keys to any vehicles.

"You can debrief me on the hows and whys later," I told Maya. "Until then, I need everyone you've got headed toward the Tower … unless you know of any other vamp hot spot in the area." I wondered if the vamps had a super-secret facility like the Feds, but given what I'd seen of the secret passages and all at the nightclub, it hardly seemed like they needed a second site.

"Gina?" Maya said suspiciously. "It's full day. Where the hell are you and how on earth are you awake? Have you been holding onto some of that formula?"—the formula the Feds had given us on the last mission that let us walk by day, if only in brief bursts.

"Where would I hide it? Everything I have, you've supplied. Whatever. Search me. But you'll have to come to the Tower to do it. Oh, and I'm not going to hang up. I'm going to leave this line open right where I am. It'll lead you to where the killer kids have holed up, where they'll probably return to if we miss them at the Tower."

"Gina, wait! I'm not done—"

But I was. I left the phone on the armrest of the couch while I tossed the cushions, earning twenty-seven cents, some butterscotch candy wrappers, and—score!—a set of keys that I hoped belonged to a vehicle that had been left behind.

Eric burst into the room. "They didn't leave much. I've got my machine and some syringes filled with water—holy, I'm guessing. I found a couple of young people strapped down in another room being bled. I set them free."

"Good."

I doubted they'd get far. The spooks were gonna want to move in fast, lock things down, debrief. But if they did manage to get away, more power to them. The fewer people I had to worry about right now, the better.

"I've got tasers and keys," I told him. "Let's see what they go to."

Eric and I found the garage we'd driven into, with only a single vehicle left inside—a little red T-top Camaro with black detailing. It was totally clear why they'd left it behind—you couldn't kidnap anyone in a Camaro. The trunk wasn't even large enough to fit a body. Don't ask me how I knew.

"Sa-weet!" I said, doing a fist-pump.

"Conspicuous," Eric answered.

"Buzzkill. Anyway, beggars/choosers and all that. Get the door. I'll drive."

"Really? And how will you survive the sunlight?"

"Damn. Okay, you drive, but don't spare the gas."

I tossed him the keys and ran back into the place for a blanket I'd seen tossed on the floor. It smelled of pizza grease, but I'd take it if it meant I didn't have to go down in a blaze of glory.

Back at the car, I laid the passenger seat down as far as it would go and wrapped myself in the blanket top to toenails.

Eric peeled out of there, and my heart clenched in fear. Ever since my death by auto accident, I was leery about racing to the rescue. It was better when I was in control, but hunkered down under the blanket, completely in the dark, the sun coming in through the windows sapping my strength, was my own personal version of hell. I was too afraid to close my eyes, even if they weren't doing me any good right then, for fear I wouldn't wake up again. Maybe ever.

"Talk to me," I ordered Eric, raising my voice to be heard outside the blanket.

"About what?" He took a corner on hyper-speed, and I swear I felt two wheels leave the road.

"Anything!" I squeaked.

"Wait until you meet Nelson. The *real* Nelson. I'm sure all this hasn't given you the best impression of him."

Oh crap, I thought *I* had problems. It hadn't even occurred to me until just then that once we rescued Eric's nephew and got him back into his real body—hopefully—he'd be facing murder charges. His face had been caught on film. He was a wanted man. Boy. Whatever. Maybe the Feds could give him a miracle makeover. Or a new identity.

"I'm sure he's, ah, very nice," I answered. It took an effort to speak. The longer we were out in the sun, the tireder I got. My body felt more stone than flesh, as if it weighed about a ton. Heavy enough to sink into oblivion.

Eric laughed without humor. "Nice doesn't really cut it. He's smart, resourceful. At three, he started taking apart everything he could find to see how it worked. Made his parents nuts. Reminded me of me. When they died ... well, death became his new obsession. Or undeath, anyway, especially when he hit his teens."

"I'm sorry."

"I feel like I failed him. I should have been able to snap him out of it."

"S'not too late," I said, my words slurred with exhaustion.

He pulled over abruptly and stopped the car. "We're here. What's the plan?"

The burn of the sun had eased up; I could tell he'd parked in the shade, but it didn't do much to revive me. I felt like I was thinking through mud, and not the therapeutic spa kind.

"What's the layout? Any sign of the Feds?"

"No, but the door is standing open. The kids are definitely inside."

"Then let's go." I did my best to go for the door handle and only managed a fevered lurch. "Except, ah, you might have to carry me." Oh yeah, I was *fierce*.

Eric came around to my side of the car, threw me over his shoulder, blanket and all, and sprinted for the front door of the Tower. The burn was almost unbearable. I felt like I had the worst temperature of my life, like I might spontaneously combust. I think the pain was all that kept me awake against the day that wanted to send me into eternal sleep. The blanket caught fire—or maybe it was me—as we hit the entrance, and Eric employed stop, drop, and roll on me. As in, stopping to shut the door behind us, dropping me to the floor, and rolling me until I was extinguished.

I lay there for a second, trying to build up the will to move. My eyes wanted desperately to close, but I fought against it.

"Where to now?" he asked.

"Office," I croaked. "I'll show you." From there, if I could get Very Scary's screens to work, we could see everything. We could pinpoint the action in an instant.

With a monumental effort, I rose, swaying as I did.

"You okay?" Eric asked.

I waited to respond until my brain decided there really was just one of him as opposed to the three I was seeing. He resolved into the one in the center. "No. I'm a nightwalker and it's day. I still can't believe I'm even wake. Don't know how long I can stay this way."

"Would blood help?"

My fangs slammed down into position, and I answered without even thinking. "Yesss." So instinct, at least, was alive and well.

Eric swallowed hard and offered a wrist. I nearly jumped on him, sinking my teeth into his lovely ripe veins. Oh, the sensation. Imagine your favorite chocolate lava cake or other indulgence and multiply the sweet sensation with a burst of pure adrenaline. Like a chocolate energy drink. Bliss.

Too soon I felt something grab at my hair, pulling me back. Reluctantly, I went, licking at my lips to collect every last drop.

I met Eric's gaze, and he looked … loopy. A bemused smile was on his face. "Ah, *now* I understand."

There was some magic to our bite that made things pleasant for the bitee. This was usually a good thing. But when the bitee was old enough to be your father … Ewk.

"Follow me," I ordered, choosing action over reaction.

I ran for the stairs. We hit the top floor at a dead run, and I risked a dislocated shoulder to bust the door into Very Scary's inner sanctum. The dazed look hadn't even faded from Eric's face by the time I got the flat-screen monitor on Very Scary's desk to pop up out of hiding and accessed the keyboard. From there I was stumped. Everything was password protected.

"Move aside," Eric ordered back. "Machines are my specialty."

His hands flew over the keys so quickly I couldn't even follow, and within seconds the wall panels had slid back to reveal the surveillance screens. Eric flipped through the screens quickly, as soon as he could determine that they weren't what he was looking for. Then we caught sight of them. Two bodies lay on the floor at the feet of the killer kids—or, at least, I could see a pair of splayed feet to the right and an elbow to the left that couldn't possibly belong to the same person … not and still be attached. But whose were they? The cameras didn't pick up the vampires, but we could see their beds and the Japanese shoji screens separating them … and the kids closing in, wooden bats once again in hand.

"Where is this?" Eric asked me, like I'd know.

I got closer to the screen he was pointing to and studied the picture, thinking fast. I almost missed the window because it was completely blacked out and the room was pretty dim to begin with, but when I looked closely, there it was, past the shoji screens—a small round window like you'd find in an...

"Attic!" I said out loud. "Top of the Tower."

"You know how to get there?"

I answered a question with a question. "Can you find us a schematic?"

His hands flew over the keys again, and he ended up with a blueprint of the place on every screen.

"Great. Now, do you know how to read it?" I asked.

He took it all in at a glance and said, "This way."

He tapped one final key on the keyboard and darted for the wall as one of Very Scary's wall panels opened before us.

I chased after him. "We're still missing a plan."

"You kick butt and find Nelson, I get everyone to safety."

"Sure, why didn't I think of that?"

He took the stairs two at a time, and then suddenly went down like a ton of bricks, landing hard as he twisted to save his precious invention rather than himself. I vaulted him to keep from going down myself, but when I turned to help, he panted, "Trip wire. I'll be okay. Just... let me catch my breath. I'll be right behind you."

I wasn't so sure of that, the way he'd fallen. I'd definitely heard the sound of bone breaking—leg, rib, I couldn't tell, but I gave him a nod. I couldn't stop now. Momentum was the only thing keeping me going.

I hit the third floor landing, and a thick plywood club, studded with nails, pointy sides out, came flying at me out of nowhere, swung like a major-league bat. I almost didn't get a hand up in time, but my vampire reflexes, even slowed, still beat any hopped-up human's. One of the nails went right through my hand, but that only guaranteed that the board was coming with me when I gave it a tug. The person on the other end—Burly Boy—came flying with it, and I sidestepped to let him take the tumble down the stairs that he'd meant for me. From his moan, I knew he'd live, even if I didn't much care at that point.

It was amazing how reviving anger and action could be. I felt my senses perking painfully as I pulled the nail from my hand and reversed my grip on the plywood so that I held the smooth part. Their weapon was now mine, and it would work on killer kids and vamps alike.

I didn't rush the next landing. I hoped they'd assume I'd gone down, as intended, and that it was Burly Boy himself headed their way.

I burst through the half-open door, slamming it back against the wall, and found myself, sure enough, in the room we'd seen onscreen, only the scene itself had changed. Or maybe I was just now able to see the missing pieces. Very Scary faced off against the killer kids, who were armed with more nail-studded bats. He stood between them and his fellow vamps, barring the way. He had to be ancient, as I'd guessed way back when by the lack of any color to his skin. Only the very oldest vamps could resist the pull of the grave when the sun came up. All the other vamps slept like what we were—the dead. The body parts I'd seen onscreen belonged, I guessed, to Very Scary's human servants, because all the killer kids were accounted for.

They turned when I crashed into the room, and the

distraction was enough for Very Scary to lunge for Nelson, lips pulled back from his fully fierce fangs and hands curved like claws. *Seriously* like claws, I realized. His nails had somehow grown like Freddy Krueger's manicurist had gotten ahold of him.

As I watched, Nelson sidestepped the attack with near-vampire speed, and Elise whirled just as quickly to strike Very Scary a blow from the seriously spiky side of her bat. He dodged that one, right into Kelly's counter-swing. Blood spurted into the air, and my own fangs came crashing down.

Behind me I heard what sounded like a rhino charging up the stairs, but had to be Burly Boy—quickly recovered, curse him, and from *my* stolen energy. I slammed the door shut behind me and put my back to it just in time to stop him from blowing through. Still, his attempt rocked me on my feet. The killer kids had already busted the lock, and the only thing standing between Burly Boy and the fight was me.

Even bloodied, Very Scary managed to dance back from two more blows coming his way and hissed at me, "You wanted to prove yourself. Now's the time."

I was torn. I *definitely* didn't want whoever was body surfing the real Nelson Ricci to win the fight. Their plan couldn't be allowed to succeed; they were too blood-thirsty. Too…psychotic. It was a dark day when Very Scary and the vamps—great name for a goth band if ever I heard one—were the lesser of two evils.

I waited for Burly Boy's next run on the door and darted out of the way, letting his momentum tumble him into the room. As he pinwheeled past, I used the less lethal side of the bat to knock him into the midst of the fight. Very Scary blurred out of the way and Kelly leapt him to come at me, a really credible growl rumbling in her throat. Burly Boy went down, taking Elise with him, but I didn't have time to see how hard they fell, as Kelly was swinging like a girl possessed.

"Come back for more?" I asked. I was still glad I hadn't drained her dead, but unconscious I could have gone for right about now.

"This time things are going to go a little differently," she spat. Her button nose made it a little hard to take her seriously, even in full snarl.

"Well then, what are you waiting for? Have at me."

I wanted her to lunge in anger rather than cold calculation, and I wasn't disappointed. It was so easy to catch her arm as I sidestepped it and whirled her into the door Burly Boy had blown through. She caught the edge of the door straight to the forehead and folded like a Macy's stock girl.

Just as I turned back to the rest of the action, the glass of the single attic window shattered inward and shards flew in every direction. I flinched away to protect my eyes and heard the sudden explosive hiss of pressurized gas releasing. I dropped low to avoid it, my flesh burning, my eyes red-hazed from blood tears, and my whole body on fire, not sure whether to implode or combust. A garlic bomb? Something else? My ears still worked, even if my eyes didn't, and I could hear retching, coughing, cries of pain from the killer kids and Very Scary alike. So, a double-edged sword then, something for everyone.

Then something else slammed through the window, landing hard and shaking the floorboards beneath my feet. I struggled to focus on what was going on and could make out a commando standing where the window had been, his face and eyes covered by a mask and goggles to protect him from the gas. He stepped aside to unhook the cord from the harness he'd ridden in on and the light coming through the shattered window hit the first of the sleeping vampires. She instantly burst into flame. Too young to actually wake, but not to let out an unholy shriek as she burned, thrashing wildly in her sleep. It was horrible, and I leapt forward to help just as the commando yanked a dagger-sized stake from a bandolier across his chest and quick as thought plunged it into her chest.

"No!" I cried, nearly unable to process what I'd just seen. The burning vampiress cut off mid-wail, convulsing around the stake before going deadly still. She hadn't been a threat. She hadn't even been *awake*.

Stunned, I stared daggers at the window warrior, but in his breathing gear, he didn't look even remotely human. He gave me a nod, as if we were on the same side, but I knew right then that we weren't. I had about a split second to prove it.

It sounded like a herd of elephants were charging up the stairs. Commando's backup, I presumed. I broke my spiky bat over my knee, ignoring the pain, and grabbed the fragments I thought to be the right size, diving for the door to slam it shut and drive the splinters in like wedges beneath it.

The commando didn't settle for just staring daggers. He apparently preferred pulling a gun, a very serious-looking rifle, from a holster on his back. Two things happened at once, then: a shoji screen that had caught fire from the flaming vampiress crashed into one of the other beds, lighting a second vampire on fire, and Very Scary started to lurch upright, recovering from the smoke bomb.

"Down!" I yelled, as the commando shifted his aim toward the new threat.

I could see the shock in his eyes, but VS obeyed almost instantly, dropping back to the floor as a bullet gouged a furrow in his scalp rather than drilling him a third eye.

The door behind me was being battered to within an inch of its life. Wood splintered. We wouldn't be alone much longer, and with Very Scary down, the commando was retraining his gun on me. Without conscious thought, I launched a final splinter from my bat at him, like a throwing knife in a circus act. At the same time, Very Scary rose up again and barreled the length of the attic to take him down. Commando fired, but Very Scary was in close enough to knock the gun aside one instant and go for his throat in the next. He never stood a chance.

The door splintered just as the killer kids, hacking up lungs, started to stagger upright, trying to escape or rejoin the fight. Feds poured into the room. I dove for the burning vampire and used my body to smother the flames.

"Stop right there!" Sid yelled.

I froze, like everyone else, guilty conscience making me check that the gun was trained on someone other than me. Commando wasn't in any condition to let them know I'd switched sides, but I was still relieved to see that it was nasty-Nelson in the crosshairs. Maya, beside Sid, covered Elise and her cohort Kelly, who was still doubled over coughing. Behind them … holy crap! They must have drawn their backup from the vampire testing facility, because one of the guys crowding their backs, all in burglar black, was Pyro's partner.

I knew the second he saw me. His eyes widened and his gun came up, high enough to aim over Maya's shoulder. "That's the girl!" he shouted.

Everyone looked at me, and while I normally liked to draw all eyes, this time I'd pass.

"What girl?" Sid asked, not as if he didn't know, but as if he wanted to be absolutely clear.

I had *one shot* at getting this right. I'd had exactly zero time to practice my newfound ability. I didn't even know for sure it was that and not a fluke, but I had to hope and pray to god or goth or *whatever* that I could pull it off.

Without waiting for the accusation I knew would come, I closed my eyes and willed myself to ghost. Whatever'd been in the commando's smoke bomb made it sting, so that I felt superheated, like steam, and it took a hair longer than it should have. Momentarily, though, I was lighter than air. I heard the commotion kick up at my disappearance—yelling, movement, confusion—but it was a distant thing, like playing telephone with tin cans. I didn't dare try to open my eyes for a look. The last time I'd tried it while ghosting, I'd fallen back into physical form.

This time, I focused on my other senses while rising above the noise and aiming to pass over the highest concentration of disturbance, figuring that would be the cavalry, and behind them stairs and freedom. When I was past it, when the air seemed … clearer, cleaner, less cluttered, I tried to sense *down*. But … hell, for all I knew, I was back in that attic, Pyro's partner had already shot me, and I was living a fever dream. I started to sink at the very thought. Ah ha—down!

Following my fall, I continued down and down, bouncing along when things seemed to get … thick. I figured those were the times when I was sinking through the stairs and did my best to rise up again. Theoretically, I probably could have ghosted right through the Tower walls and out, but that way lay daylight and death.

Then something rushed through me from behind, shocking me back into myself, and suddenly I was solid and stumbling. I grabbed for anything I could use to break my fall and latched onto a pair of serious shoulders, sending us both boobs-over-booty down the stairs. My boobs, anyway, his booty, since clearly I was holding on to a guy. The only woman I knew with shoulders like that was Chickzilla, and I'd left her back in Ohio with smelly Melli—Bobby's sucky siress. We didn't get far before we hit a landing, and even though I was pretty certain I was on the bottom, I'd fallen on something soft that *oofed* as I hit.

But I didn't have time to analyze that before my partner came down on top of me. Oh crap...make that *Pyro's* partner. Now that we'd stopped spinning, I could see that was exactly who was snarling down at me. He'd lost his gun, but he had his weight, pinning me down. He didn't need much else. I'd about exhausted my resources.

"I'll kill you," he spat in my face. Literally, it was more spray than say.

"No, you won't," said the pillow I'd landed on—*Eric?* I craned my neck to look, relieved that someone was finally on *my* side, even if he hadn't been "right behind" me as he'd promised.

Yes, Eric—still clutching his machine to his chest, still right where he'd fallen. He took in the situation in an instant and reached out to Pyro's partner, flipping a switch on his machine. I watched as the thug went as stiff as a board, and then relaxed by degrees as all his vitality seeped out of him. When he'd sagged, Eric took his hand back, set his machine down, and lifted me and my dead weight right off him like he'd suddenly become Superman. Whatever had kept him down, it seemed that Pyro's partner's energy had temporarily counteracted it.

"Nelson?" he asked.

"The Feds have the place locked down. He'll be fine until we can steal him away." I thought about the facility Eric had shown me ... "For now. But we have to get out of here."

"I can't leave him here."

On the floor above us, it sounded like they were moving furniture ... or bodies. Someone else would be coming our way any second.

"Well, I can," I said. "You can either fight the Feds on your own and lose, or you can fall back with me and live to fight another day. Even as strong as you are now, you can't take all of them."

He looked up, as if he could see through the furiously creaking floorboards. "Let's go."

We ran, but not without his precious machine. Never that.

We were all the way to the lobby of the Tower before I realized it wasn't going to be as easy as making a quick getaway. If the Feds had any sense at all—and, sadly, they did—they were going to be watching entrances and exits. We were parked right out front. There was no safe way to go back to the Camaro, as sweet as it was. How, then, were we getting away? How were we even getting out? I might be able to ghost ... maybe, if it didn't take strength and concentration, which I was fast running out of ... but that wouldn't do a thing for Eric.

"Eric, you're going to have to save yourself," I told him. "I'm trapped until night."

"There's no way you can hold out that long. They'll capture you."

"No, they won't." But it was a knee-jerk reaction. I didn't really have a plan. We'd left the schematic up on Very Scary's computer. There was no place I could hide where the Feds couldn't find me. Unless... "Eric, do you have one of those photogenic memories?"

He looked baffled. "You mean photographic?"

"Yeah, whatever. Potato, potah-to. Do you?"

"Yes, but—"

"Can you tell me where the Tower stores its kegs?"

His face cleared of confusion and he quickly sketched out where I should go.

"Give me a sec to get away," I ordered, "then launch a barstool through one window as a distraction and get out through another. Stay away from anywhere the Feds might think to look for you, and get in touch with..." Crap, what was Marcy's undercover name? Stacy... Stacy... "*Santos*, that's it! Look up Stacy Santos. She hangs with the steampunk crowd here. You'll probably have to leave her a message. Have her round up whoever she can and meet me here as soon as possible after dark. We're going to get your nephew back." And take down the Feds' hospital of horrors while we were at it.

"I'm coming too."

"Whatever floats your boat."

Footsteps sounded like they were coming through the ceiling. Our time was up. "Go!"

16

I didn't see Eric escape or the Feds tearing the place apart. It had been all I could do—at five foot nothing and a hundred pounds dripping wet, with daylight draining my vamp strength—to roll one of the empty kegs over to the others that hadn't yet been tapped and to ghost inside. Going solid again all pretzeled up hadn't exactly been comfortable, but I'd only been aware of it for seconds before sleep knocked me over the head and dragged me off to its dark lair of oblivion.

I jerked awake as usual at sunset, panicking at the enclosed space, feeling myself back in the grave, in my coffin, having to fight my way out. But then my brain caught up with me. I remembered the keg and the chaos ... and the ghosting. It had been for real, then. I'd finally found my superpower. Go me.

I was still weak from being drained by the killer kids and unnaturally active by day ... not to mention all the action I'd seen. It took everything I had to ghost out of the keg, smelling like an entire brewery. I was totally craving the blood of a caffeine addict, but I didn't have time to go hunting and was still worried about feeding out of need. If I got through this, I was going to have to set myself on some kind of diet regimen. Regular meals. Spare blood I could down like an energy drink. I licked my lips and ended up grazing my tongue on a fang.

Darn it, I had to *focus*. My backup would be here soon. I needed a plan, and I needed weapons. The Feds had tossed the taproom pretty well, looking for me, but it wasn't until I moved into the main part of the club that I saw how thorough they'd been. The windows Eric had smashed to escape were still open to the night, letting in sticky-humid air. But those weren't the only ugly holes dotting the walls. The Feds had made a few of their own, probably where they'd sensed hollow spots. Furniture had been displaced, overturned, or even ripped into. Chairs were belly up, legs in the air like dead bugs scattered across the floor.

There was nothing for me here. I went to Very Scary's office to check the schematic, hoping for a place helpfully labeled *arsenal*, but the Feds had, of course, raided the room and taken the computer. With nothing better to do at the moment, I conducted my own search of the office. I could make myself brass knuckles out of paperclips, but that was about all they'd left me. Or ... wait. I came up with a silver letter-opener shaped like a dagger. It was tiny, but I tucked it into my cleavage. It might come in handy ... if I ever needed to fight something smaller than a breadbox.

I hoped the others arrived better armed and with enough to share.

I didn't have long to wait.

We're here, Bobby said in my head—I guess so they wouldn't startle me with their arrival. I met him at the first floor bar area, amid the devastation.

Before I could even take them all in, Bobby grabbed me and held me to his very nice chest. I was happy to stay there for a minute, running my hands over his back and just breathing in his scent. He'd been in such a rush, he hadn't taken a shower before coming to my call. It made sense—kick butt first, shower later. Beating on baddies did tend to get your hands dirty, not to mention the rest of you. The point was that he smelled good ... he smelled like *him*. There was a spicy, tangy scent to the blood roaring through his veins that made me want to take a bite out of him and then let him return the favor. I nuzzled the pulse point of his neck, teasing him with just the tips of my teeth, which had, of course, grown at the smell of him.

"*Now* do you believe me?" I asked, not totally able to let it go.

Bobby gazed down at me like he was a dying man lost in the desert and I was a sudden oasis. "Always. I never seriously doubted you. I just had to wrap my head around it. And when Sid and Maya declared you public enemy number one ... I knew whose side I was on."

Then my brainy boy ran out of words and used his lips to

show me exactly which side that was, sipping from me like I was that oasis and he'd been days without drink.

Then two hands yanked us apart and Eric stood there glaring. "Can we maybe save my nephew first, snog later?"

Bobby's eyes were blue flame and still on me. "Later," he promised.

"You'd better believe it."

Reluctantly, I put off the idea of riding off into the sunset for a moonlit makeout session and turned to the others.

My heart almost gave out, which wouldn't, for me, have been that catastrophic, but I kinda wanted to keep it for moments like this. I had minions! Like, *seriously*.

It wasn't just Marcy, who I'd been expecting, although ... maybe not dressed just like *that*. It was Brent and Eric too. But Marcy was the one who demanded my attention. She looked like the bastard love child of Rambo and a retro Miss America, except that her sash was a bandolier or whatever you called those things you always saw crisscrossing the hunky hero's chest in action movies. It was fully loaded with ammo. Her dark, stick-straight hair was pulled back into a sleek club at the base of her neck. She looked beautiful and deadly. From the expression on Brent's face, that was a pretty potent combo. In fact, he looked so shell-shocked I wondered if she'd already field-tested her ammo.

"What are you wearing?" I asked.

"My doomsday dress! Do you like it?" She spun and stopped with one leg cocked, striking a pose to offer up her most flattering angle. Stomach in, chest out. "We finished it last night, though I made some modifications on my own."

She unhooked a piece of hardware from her sash to show me.

"Is that a grenade?" I asked, not daring to touch it.

"A live one," she answered proudly. "All you have to do is pull the pin—"

"Don't!" Eric and Brent said at the same time.

She pouted. "Spoilsports."

I turned to Brent, giving him the hairy eyeball and waiting for him to flinch. "What about *him?* He's one of them. How do we know we can trust him not to turn on us?"

Marcy's hand and Brent's magically found each other and held tight. "Because I said so," she answered, giving me a stink-eye all her own. Girlfriend could *glare* like the setting sun off a rearview mirror.

My lips twitched. *About damn time those two figured it out.*

"Good enough for me. *But*," I said, not yet ready to release Brent when I had him on the hook, "if you betray us or hurt my friend in any way, you die a horrible death. Got it?"

He smiled and kissed the hand he held, giving Marcy a look hot enough to burn the place to the ground. "You don't have to worry about me."

"Fine," I said, finding I actually had to swallow around a lump in my throat. "Do we have a plan?"

As it turns out, we did.

We loaded up into the *olds*mobile Eric had managed to secure. Bobby, with his long legs, was riding shotgun, and I was crammed in the back on the hump between the two love birds, who were about to light the car on fire with their smoldering glances. It was hard to hold on to the feeling of being badass while sitting in the kiddy seat, feet propped up on the center bump and knees almost to my chin.

Eric parked almost exactly where I'd had Hunter park before. We traveled through the tall grass toward the "closed" clinic as silently as we possibly could. It made sense that's where the Feds would have taken everyone—the vamps at the very least—to be strapped to beds and bled. At least they weren't in possession of Eric's machine. He'd rescued that. But they knew about it. I doubted they'd simply let it walk away. Or its creator. But Eric had apparently become one of my people, and I wasn't going to let him get got.

In short order, we stood approximately where Eric and I had met the other night. He'd already told the others about my spankin' new power, and thus I was totally the lynchpin of the plan they'd worked out. If I didn't do my part, no one else could do theirs. I gave Bobby a good-bye-for-now kiss, a lingering one. He nipped at my lower lip, and all I wanted to do was stand there forever with him, but I pulled back before Eric could clear his throat or otherwise give us away. I had to step apart from Bobby to focus on being insubstantial, invisible, untouchable. Otherwise, I'd stay too aware of my body. It took an extra second or two before I felt all ghostly. I heard Marcy gasp in awe. Maybe someday with enough practice I'd learn to pull this off with my eyes open. I'd love to have seen the expression on her face.

I rose like hot air until I could sense the top of the fence from the way the breeze now seemed to strike me from a new direction. The others were going to give me until the count of three before they started their diversionary mayhem to pull the guards away from their posts so that I could materialize inside the facility to wreak my own havoc, disassembling the security system so they could storm the clinic. I floated across the grounds, going from memory toward the clinic, hoping to enter at just the right place.

I felt the explosions outside the wall begin, like shock waves ripping through me, threatening to scatter me to the wind.

Then the unthinkable happened. Some kind of security measure triggered, and suddenly I was thrown back into physical form and pinned to the ground by daylight. No, that couldn't be possible. It was full night. But … oh crap, these weren't searchlights that had come on. *They were sunlamps.* My vinyl dress didn't so much go up in flame as begin to melt into me, searing into my flesh as if it would become my new candy coating. Guards rushed past from inside—two, four, more— and I held my scream to stay unnoticed. My only hope was to get through those doors before they closed behind the guards. I couldn't do that if I was being tackled and shackled.

I used the pain, the fear, the burning, everything I had to motivate myself into overdrive. The world was a blur as I flew into action, diving at the doors and skidding on my belly through them as they closed. I left a smear of vinyl. My dress tore, but it was the least of my worries. Heedless of anyone who might be watching, I rolled momentarily on the cool tile, extinguishing the flames. My boots had all but melted, the black soles leaving more streak marks behind on the tile. Served them right.

I was in the emergency room foyer. I'd gotten that much right. Getting to my feet, body crying out with every movement, I saw that my minions had done their jobs with the grenades. The surveillance post was deserted. I hoped my peeps were out of reach of the horrible light and prayed my part wouldn't come too late to save them if not.

I pulled the cell phone–sized device Eric had given me from my cleavage, the only place I'd had to store it. There were three silver buttons on top of its matte black exterior that had to be hit in the right sequence. He'd shown me, and I did it now, placing the device on the ledge of the security window and cringing away as if it might hurt me, even though Eric promised it wouldn't.

It sent out a pulse that I felt almost the same way I felt Bobby's powers. It seemed to echo through my blood and bones.

And then everything went dark. *Everything*. All the lights, inside and outside, the screens behind the security desk. Everything that ran on electricity. Eric had called the device a portable electromagnetic pulse—EMP—transmitter, sure to knock out any electronics within a small sphere like this building.

Now that full darkness had returned I could think clearly again. *Lights out* was the signal for the others to move in. They'd know instantly that Eric's mini-machine had worked. It was time for part two of the plan ... free the vamp body that Nelson was trapped in, along with all the other vamps the Feds had collected from the Tower. Bobby and the rest of my teammates would keep the guards busy and secure our escape route.

With the electronics fried, there was no way to open the inner door, and the glass of the security window was sure to be bulletproof. The only way in was *through*. It had been freaky enough the times I'd stupidly almost fallen through objects, like the stairs back at the Tower. I'd felt dense, heavy, like something else's mass was combining with mine. I had a horrible fear that if I lost focus … or maybe gained it, even for a second … I might not get sorted out again. I mean, machine parts were all well and good for Iron Man, but for me … Well, hey, if I became a clockwork girl, at least I'd be a shoe-in for the Burgess Brigade.

Anyway, I had no choice. I grabbed hold of my sense of self and concentrated on being *me*, but less physical. Me as a spiritual being. My old gang would laugh themselves silly at the thought. But the joke would be on them, because I was lighter than air, lighter even than a carb-starved supermodel.

I took a figurative breath and launched myself through the inner door. There was that moment of thickness, where I felt caught and held fast, a fly in amber, then I pulled free and was out again. If I'd still been human or, you know, embodied, I'd be hyperventilating. But panic wasn't on my agenda. Rescue was.

I came back to myself on the other side, needing my actual senses to scope things out. I knew the general layout from my other invasion, but I didn't know—ah ha! Down the right-hand corridor, two of the doors were ajar. Evidently they hadn't been shut at the time of the pulse. I'd start there. If those rooms were occupied and I could free their occupants first, I'd have built-in backup. I wouldn't be battering in doors all by my lonesome. Because how wrong was it that I now had minions but was totally still on my own?

The hallway was clear, but I didn't know for how long. In my last pass-through, I'd seen how much security they had on staff, and I knew I hadn't seen enough of them run by me while I was burning near to death to empty the place out. I had to act fast.

I bolted for the closest open door off the corridor. Immediately, something pierced my arm, and I looked down to see a hypodermic needle sticking out of my flesh. I raised my glance from the needle to the fear-crazed eyes of the white-coated guy who'd jabbed me with it, and I swear he nearly wet himself at the look on my face. He made a sudden move to my right, but with a human facing down a vamp, "sudden" was a relative term. He didn't have a prayer. I grabbed him by both shoulders and threw him to the ground, leaping on top of him. I forced him to look at me.

"What was in the needle?" I growled.

"N-n-nothing. Just a needle from my cart. I'm a phlebotomist."

"A what?"

"A blood guy," came a chill voice from one of the two beds in the small room. *I knew* that voice.

"Selene?"

"Just snap his neck and be done with it," she answered. "You bust us out and you're in. You've proven yourself."

Oh, right. She had no idea my mission had been called on account of conscience.

The blood-boy squirmed and thrashed and did his level best to escape, but there was no way I was killing anyone. Not if I could help it. Someone who went around sticking other people for blood surely wouldn't mind a donation of his own. After all, didn't they say that charity begins at home?

My teeth were already down with that thought. I caught a whiff of him as I lowered my lips to his neck. Fear, as intoxicating as it might be, did not do good things for a man's scent. Not generally. But I forgot all that when my teeth pierced the flesh of his neck, and his hot, sweet blood came pouring out. I didn't lose myself this time. I was way too conscious of the ticking clock. I took just enough to feel my burns begin to heal and the exhaustion of the past few days slip away. I felt more energized. More superhuman. More *me*. If only the blood would do the same for my clothes.

When I pulled back, I dealt him a blow to the head where I'd learned in training it would do the most good. He wouldn't be coming after us or raising any alarms, but he'd live.

I raced to Selene's bedside and began undoing her straps. As soon as her hands were free, she started ripping needles and tubing out of her arms. I got to work on her leg restraints.

"I've got this," she said. "You just take care of Zzz— uh, Xavier."

It wasn't what she'd meant to say, I'd stake my whole collection of Dolce & Gabbana on it. The list of names starting with the Z sound was pretty short. In fact, I could think of only one other, more of a nickname, really—*Xander*.

I looked over at the other table, but the vamp there seemed glassy-eyed. Not all bright-eyed and bushy-fanged like I expected fellow vamps to be this time of night. I approached his bed and started on his restraints, using the excuse to lean in and whisper, hopefully too quietly for Selene to hear, "*Nelson?*" She didn't want me to know who I had, and that made me suspicious.

His eyes focused on me, but the befuddlement didn't clear, which made total sense, since I was a complete stranger in a melted vinyl dress, smelling like a killer cocktail of car tire and char.

"Who—?" I could practically hear his lips crack as they opened and wondered how long it had been since he'd fed. With a body that big, he'd totally need to feed on a regular basis. He was about the size of a basketball player, with the pro-ball buzz-cut cookin' too. Reddish brown hair grew right into sideburns that in turn led into a closely shaved chinstrap beard. Handsome in a totally Cro-Magnon sort of way.

"Your uncle sent me," I whispered, falling silent just as Selene appeared beside me, staring down at Nelson like he was the cherry on her sundae and she could just eat him up, which totally grossed me out, because she probably had, like, a century on him at the very least. Talk about cougar. But I guess that was only if she wanted him for his mind … the current one. She'd called him Xander … or just kept herself from calling him that, anyway. I was pretty sure that was who she saw when she looked at him, even knowing that he was currently body-swapped.

Selene tore at the bonds around his legs, then helped him to stand, gripping him tightly.

"Let's go," I said, turning away from the confusion and fear in Nelson's eyes. Now was not the time to confront Selene. Later, in the confusion of the escape, the two could easily be separated. Permanently.

I got to the doorway first and looked both ways, ducking quickly back inside as two guards in goggles that made them look like ant aliens turned onto the hall. Night-vision goggles. Crap. Eric had warned me that anything turned off and stowed in their upright and locked position would survive the EMP.

"We've been spotted!" I cried, but quietly, just in case I was wrong. "Grab something to use as a weapon." Because no way was I surrendering any of mine. Not that I didn't trust Selene...to stab me in the back.

There was no time to think beyond that. In a blink, the two alien-thugs were in the doorway, aiming pistols our way. I was counting on wooden bullets and on not getting hit. Also, winning the lottery, regaining my reflection, and becoming a Victoria's Secret model...not necessarily in that order. I kicked the gun hand of the first guy, even as he fired. His shot went high, but he kept hold of the gun and was already lowering it for a second shot.

Nelson/Xander reached right over me and ripped the gun out of his hand, turning it back on the thug. The other one used his partner's shoulder as a stabilizer and fired off a shot, zinging the gun straight out of Nelson's hand. It flew into the air. While thug one winced from the sound of the gunshot going off in his ear, I brought a knee up hard into his groin. His dangly bits were no match for my nicely-shaped knees, and he went down like the loser in a drunken game of Twister, leaving thug two totally exposed.

He re-aimed his pistol at me—clearly the bigger threat since I'd just downed his pal. Selene finally entered the fight, whirling an IV pole over my head and whacking the last thug standing in the temple. His head cracked ominously, and he fell to the ground like Humpty Dumpty off the wall.

I frisked him quickly for weapons, thinking twice before finally deciding to arm Selene. "The only way out is with me," I told her, fixing her with the hairy-eyeball and loading any mesmeric mojo I might have into the statement. "I have a team outside. You're either with us or you're dead."

Nelson grabbed the second gun off the floor where it had gone flying. He was kind of awkward in his movement—gawky as though he'd just gone through a growth spurt and didn't yet know how to handle his arms and legs, which made sense if he was walking around in someone else's body—especially if he hadn't had a lot of practice at it because the vamps had kept him hungry or locked away. At least, it seemed, I could trust Selene where he was concerned. She'd look after his body, if not his soul.

I peeked into the hall, and this time found the coast clear. There was a door straight across the way. If we could get a good running start, with our vamp speed and power we should be able to bust it down. But we couldn't all hit the door at once. There wasn't room. As the most petite, and the boss besides...I delegated.

"You two, bust down that door. Bust down as many as you can. I'm going to get us reinforcements."

Nelson nodded. Selene looked more dubious about my authority, but finally nodded as well, which was good, because kicking her butt would take time I wasn't sure we had. I dashed down the hall to the next open door and was just inside when I heard them slam into the room opposite.

No one jumped me this time, and I could see why in an instant. A lab coat guy...no, *gal* this time, at least if the long red hair was anything to go by...must have gotten too close to one of the vamps on the gurneys. Whether the vamp had mesmerized her or she'd just been careless, it was clearly the last mistake she'd ever make. I couldn't see her face through all the hair, but I could see her throat—what was left of it.

I looked into the eyes of the vampire responsible and realized that the name *Very Scary* was clearly an understatement. Homicidal. Psychopathic. *Evil.* Any of those would have been a lot more accurate. I tried to think whether under the same conditions—trapped, fighting for the strength to break free—I would have torn out a woman's throat. The blood I'd taken from her fellow tech curdled in my stomach. No. Never. Not even if I'd been starved to the point of feral. Kelly Swinter had survived, after all.

I tore my gaze away from those eyes that glittered like snake venom and turned to the vamp on the other bed in the room. I didn't recognize him, but at this point I was perfectly willing to take the devil I didn't know over the one I did. I freed his bonds and he dashed to Very Scary's side.

"*Don't*," I ordered, leveling the guard's gun at him. "You're with me. We're freeing the others."

His eyes widened as he turned back at my command and spotted my gun. "But what about—"

"Leave him." I was bluffing with the gun, I was almost sure of it. Shooting him wouldn't be any better than what Very Scary had done to the girl. Unless the wound *I* inflicted was non-lethal.

Very Scary rattled his gurney, making a helluva racket trying to free himself. "You're still thinking like a human," he spat. "It's us against them."

"Right now, I don't want to claim either of you," I told him with perfect honesty. I waved my gun at the other vamp. "Move."

With a single glance back at Very Scary, he moved off into the hall, where Selene and Nelson had managed to free two others. Down the end of the corridor, toward the entrance, I heard shouting and more explosions. It sounded like the battle was still going full force. But we had a growing army now, and the Federal flunkies would soon be sandwiched between the vamps and our small band of rebels.

I picked the two biggest vamps besides Nelson-Xander, who was already rubbing his door-bashing shoulder. "You two, keep banging down doors and freeing the others. *Do not* let your leader loose or you answer to me."

They looked at each other, probably wondering why they were taking orders from a green girl half their size, but "escape" must have registered with them. Either that or I was far more intimidating than I thought.

"The rest of you, come with me."

We headed toward rather than away from the noise and found the hospital guards falling back to the entrance. There were a dozen or so still standing, but they were bloodied. The guards in the back turned at our approach. The closest, real-izing attack would be coming from both sides now, gave a cry, dropped his weapon, and dropped to the floor himself, assum-ing a non-threatening position with arms spread. His closest compatriot saw this and twisted his face up with disgust. He wasn't going down that easily. He yelled something unflatter-ing and started firing at us. Too high to hit me—one advantage of being short—but behind me someone gasped and stumbled back. The others roared around me like a tidal wave, rushing the hero guard and taking him down, spraying bullets as he went. The hulk that was Nelson grunted and jerked with the impact of a round to the shoulder, but kept on going. Other cries of pain nearly drowned out the sound of gunfire, and I rushed in, elbowing a guard in the gut as he raised a rifle to fire on Selene, who had her back to him dealing with one of his pals. I got in under his guard, and as he *oophed*, I used all my weight to wrench his gun from him.

Out of nowhere came a blow to my lower back with a gun butt, and I fell forward, through a sudden gap in the guards. I would have gone sprawling on my face if Bobby hadn't caught me. I smiled fiercely. Glad to see him, glad I'd fought my way through. Fell through. Same difference. We turned as one, shoulder to shoulder to meet the remaining resistance, but it was short-lived. The Feds were down to less than half the remaining flunkies—few enough that Bobby was able to dis-arm them all with one great Jedi mind trick ... or anyway, tele-kinetic blow to their weaponry. Guns clattered to the floor and hands went up. In some cases only one hand, as the other put pressure on a war wound.

"Lock them up," I ordered the vamps still standing.

Selene stepped to the front, hands on her hips and eyes blazing cold fire. "Just a second. Who made you boss? You don't get to decide to leave the master behind. We don't take orders—"

A sound like a hive of pissed-off wasps broke in on her, and suddenly she froze, her eyes rolling up into her head. She fell jittering to the floor.

Hulk-Nelson stood behind her, holding a taser he must have taken off one of the guards.

"I've had enough of her," he said, glaring around. "Any-body else?"

No one else seemed inclined to step up, at least not at that moment. The freed vamps started rounding up the guards and taking them back to the newly empty rooms for lockup.

Nelson stayed in place, now staring at me in challenge.

"They can't have it back," he said, giving me a look that dared me to argue.

I didn't even blink. You didn't look away from a potential nutbar with a taser. "Have what back?" I asked.

"This body. They've ruined mine. They locked me away, but I heard everything. I know my face has been splashed all over the media. I'm a wanted man. Xander did the crime, he can do the time."

Bobby came up to stand beside me. Then Marcy and Brent. If he tried to come at me with that taser, he wouldn't get far. Hell, Bobby could drop him where he stood. But after all he'd been through ...

"That seems fair," I told him.

His stance eased a little ... until the sirens started off in the distance, until a new figure stepped through the outer door and said, "The police are on their way. We'd better get going."

"Uncle Eric?" Nelson asked, wonder in his voice. His face went through a complete transformation, and remarkably I could see the teen boy inside. He dropped the taser.

"Nelson?" Eric asked back. "Is that really you?

They rushed at each other, and suddenly there was a big old hugfest right there in the entryway with freed vamps streaming around us, running off before the sirens could get any closer.

"Guys," Brent cut in, "can we put the family reunion on hold? We'd better get out of here right flippin' now."

"But we can't just leave this place to start right up again once we're gone," I protested.

"I don't think that's going to be a problem," Marcy said. "We destroyed most of the fence. The vamps probably destroyed the rest on their way out. And now that they know it's here..."

"The Feds'll just start fresh somewhere else," I said with a sigh.

"Nothing we can do about that tonight," Brent answered. "Let's move."

We raced off into the night, leaving the authorities to clean up our mess.

17

Brent hot-wired us a van from the hospital lot—a much roomier ride than we'd had on the way over—and we rushed to escape the area before any kind of perimeter could be set up. If the area went into lockdown, if the state or local authorities set up roadblocks and checkpoints, we'd be toast.

Eric took some crazy chances and ran at least three red lights. I wouldn't have given him credit for having the balls, but I had to admit, I was pretty impressed—*terrified*, but impressed. It wasn't until he finally slowed and started driving like a law-abiding citizen that it occurred to me that we'd destroyed a lot more than a Federal facility. We'd pretty much blown up our past, present, and future. We couldn't go back…not to Mozulla, Ohio, not to the Hudson Valley of New York, and now not to anywhere near Tampa, Florida. The Feds would be looking for us, probably with homicidal intent. Was there anywhere we'd be safe?

"Uh, guys?" I said into the silence. "What now?"

"Well, I thought we'd head back to my hideout," Eric answered. "No one's found it yet, and you should be safe—"

"No, I mean what *next*? Not where do we go to ground for a day, but after that."

We'd gone from high school, which at least had some end in sight, to the potential of eternity tangled up in vampire power plays, to an offer we couldn't refuse to work for the Feds. As long as I'd been alive, someone had insisted I do this or that. Sure, I did it my way, in style, but still…Now we had all the freedom a price on our heads would allow and no direction. Kinda like having a degree but no idea what to do with the rest of your life, and we had a helluva lot of it in front of us. It was…scary. Maybe scarier than anything else we'd faced so far.

"That's a good question," Brent said, squeezing Marcy's hand. "You have an idea?"

"I do," Bobby cut in. Everybody but Eric looked at him expectantly. "This isn't over—this Cold War or whatever between the Fangs and the Feds—and both are messing with civilians."

"Civilians?" Brent asked.

"Yeah, like I was before the Feds sucked me in, before I met you," Marcy said, bumping him with her shoulder. He bumped her back, and before long it devolved into rolling around on the floor of the van in a liplock of epic proportions—moaning, groping, and rubbing up against each other. Hot enough to get them a PG-13 rating. Bobby and I looked at each other and exchanged a smoldering glance of our own. We had ideas, but they'd keep. We could totally be the mature ones.

"You were saying," I prompted Bobby, trying to ignore my bestie and her new boy toy as they rolled into my leg.

"Look, we might have busted into that hospital to rescue Nelson, but we busted the others out because what the Feds were doing was *wrong*. But now, whatever the vamps do— whether they find a way to overcome their sunlight sensitivity or mesmerize people to line up to be lunch... it's on us."

Well, crap. "So what do you propose we do about it?"

"There must be other sites, right? Other places, other states, other facilities. We find them and we shut them down."

"Us against the Feds?" Marcy asked dubiously.

"*And* the vamps. Think about it like checks and balances on the whole thing."

"Like what?"

"You know, like the three branches of government are each supposed to keep watch on the others. We keep an eye on the Fangs and the Feds and step in where we're needed."

"Oh, the Fangs *and* the Feds," Marcy answered. "That's *much* better."

"I'm in," Nelson said instantly.

Eric almost veered off the road. "You sure about that? You've only just gotten your life back—"

"After everything they did to me... Yeah, I'm sure. But only if you're with us."

"I—crud puppies!" Eric cursed, suddenly slowing down to a crawl. He stared off to the left, down a side street we were creeping past. Halfway down the block was a cluster of cars, all dark. No bells or whistles, but one of them had a light bar on top. Patrol unit, no doubt. A small army of men swarmed from them in dark suits or crime-scene-tech coveralls. "They found where I've been staying. I thought we'd be safe there, but ... "

"I know where we can go," I said. "Or at least who we can call." All eyes were on me now, which was as it should be. "Anybody got a cell phone?"

Brent produced one from his pocket, surprisingly not crushed into dust with all the rolling around he'd just been doing with Marcy.

I raised a brow at him. "A disposable," he said. "Not Federal issue."

"Great." I still remembered Hunter's number. Maybe all the super spy training had finally taken ... just in time for me to use it against them.

The call went through and the phone started to ring. I knew I could count on Hunter's help, as long as I was willing to pay the price. All it would take was one little kiss ... the eternal kind.

"So, where do we want to start?" I asked as I waited for the call to connect.

"Vegas," Eric offered.

"L.A.," Marcy chirped.

"Somewhere a lot less sunshiny," Bobby suggested. "Maybe the Pacific Northwest."

"Salem, Massachusetts," Brent said. "We'll blend right in."

Hunter came on the line and we arranged to meet. Tonight we'd get the hell out of Dodge. Tomorrow we'd take on the world.

The End.

About the Author

Lucienne Diver writes humorous vamps, because it's hard to take life seriously when your puppy sits under your desk licking your toes as you type. Her heroine, Gina, got her start in *Vamped* and, as will come as no surprise to those who've read it, subsequently decided she wanted more, more, MORE! Thus, one book became two and two will become four—who knows where it will stop? Today the book store, tomorrow the mall!

Stay tuned for the further adventures of the Covello Clan in Fangtabulous, *forthcoming from Flux Books!*